Beverley Naidoo

CHAIN OF FIRE

Editor: E. S. Odland
Illustrations: Naja Abelsen

D1664482

EASY READERS

ER

EASY READERS

The vocabulary is based on
Michael West: A General Service List of
English Words, revised & enlarged edition 1953
Pacemaker Core Vocabulary, 1975
Salling/Hvid: English-Danish Basic Dictionary, 1970
J. A. van Ek: The Threshold Level for Modern Language
Learning in Schools, 1976

Series editor: Ulla Malmmose

Cover layout: Mette Plesner

Printed in Denmark by
Sangill Grafisk Produktion, Holme-Olstrup

BIOGRAPHY

Beverley Naidoo grew up in South Africa under the apartheid* regime. At the age of 21 she was detained without trial on account of her political views. Naidoo left South Africa the following year for Britain, where she has since lived.

Her first book about Naledi and her family, 'Journey to Jo'burg', won the Child Study Children's Book Award, given by Bank Street College, in 1986.

Notes:
Apartheid means separation. It was a political system in which people of different races were separated.

Nelson Mandela, born 1918, South African statesman, President since 1994, shared the Nobel Peace Prize with Frederik de Klerk in 1993.

South Africa = The South African Republic since 1961. From 1910-1961 it was called The South African Union and was a dominion of the British Commonwealth.

Official languages: Afrikaans and English.

The most important African languages: Xhosa, Zuli, Sesotho.

Chapter 1

"Come over here, Naledi! Look here!"

Tiro stared at the number 1427 written in fresh white paint across the door of their house. He was on his way out to the village *tap* to *collect* the morning's water. The paint was still wet. He turned to Naledi, his fifteen-year-old sister. Fear showed in her dark eyes.

"Who did this, Naledi? We didn't hear anything!"

Their four-year-old sister, Dineo jumped up trying to touch the paint.

Pulling the child gently away from the door, Naledi held her small hand as they ran out to the low *mud* wall that was around the yard.

"That's the one!"

Tiro looked down the *track* of the village road. In the distance was a man carrying a *brush*. A group of people was gathering. The man seemed to be backing away. Still holding Dineo's hand, Naledi began to run up the track. Tiro, eleven years old and with strong legs, soon ran ahead. Large white numbers were painted on the doors of the other houses they passed. As they got closer, they could hear their *neighbour* **Mma*** Tshadi's voice rising above the rest. Her large arms seemed to be push-

---

collect [kə'lekt], to come for and take away; to come together or bring people or things together
mud, soft wet earth that becomes hard when it dries
track, a line or series of marks left by a moving car, person, animal or the like
brush, see picture, page
gather ['gæðə], to get together
neighbour ['neɪbə], a person living next to or near another
*Mrs; Madam; mother

4

tap

bucket

ing the man backwards.

"Don't you touch my house!"

"Mma ... excuse me... It's not my wish. It's the government's wish. The government **baas*** says I must put the numbers on all the houses here." 5

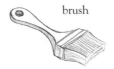

brush

*boss

He pulled out some paper from his pocket, but quickly put it back as Mma Tshadi put out her hand to take it. At that moment the sound of a car caused everyone to turn. A blue car came forward slowly from behind the small stone church building up the road. Two white men in suits climbed out.

"What's the trouble, then?" asked one of them in English.

"This lady ... she doesn't want me to put the number on her door, baas."

He seemed to stand a little taller, now that his 'boss' was with him. He even spoke in English, not in Tswana.

"Don't you people know you have to move from here?" the man from the car said. "The *trucks* will come for you in four weeks' time. So that's why you must have numbers on your houses. Then the whole thing can be done in a proper way and there won't be any *upsets*."

"What do you mean 'move from here'? These are our homes. We live here. What do you mean 'trucks are coming'?" Mma Tsadi said.

Naledi's heart beat fast. This white man must be from 'Affairs', from the Government, but Mma Tshadi wasn't afraid to talk back to him. Younger than their grandmother Nono, she was a large woman with a voice that had always been *loud*. The man from 'Affairs' now looked directly at Mma Tshadi.

---

truck, a big car which is open at the back, used for transporting goods
upset, to make somebody unhappy or worried; to bring out of order; the state of being so
loud, easily heard; producing much noise

6

"Do you pay rent to Chief Sekete?"

Mma Tshadi *nodded*.

"Well, if you don't know about the move, that's not our *fault*. The landowners here, Chief Sekete and his family, were informed long ago. In fact, your chief has seen the place where you're going. I even heard him say that it's better than here. So you must ask him, not us. Now let my boy get on with his job painting up the numbers."

He looked over at the man with the paint.

"Hurry up, John. We haven't got all day."

Quiet with shock, the group stood watching as the man hurried up the *path* to Mma Tshadi's house and put a number across the door... 1438. Then he made his way across to the next house... 1439... and the next. Saying nothing, Mma Tshadi set off, followed by the others, in the direction of Chief Sekete's house.

Chapter 2

"What does he mean... trucks are coming for us in four weeks' time? To go where?" Tiro's eyes were worried, his voice angry. "Let's go with Mma Tshadi to find out."

He pulled Naledi's arm but she held back. She was thinking of their grandmother, in whose house they all lived.

"No, I must tell Nono first. You go with them."

As Tiro hurried after the others, Naledi looked at the two white men standing by the car. They were looking

nod, to move the head up and down to say 'yes'
fault [fɔːlt], responsibility for something wrong
path, a way made by or for people walking

7

around at the village. Its houses, most of them with walls made of mud, were spread out over an area of dry *grass* along paths of earth on a *slope* down to the flat *veld*. The white men seemed so sure of themselves. What right did they have to come like this? Naledi took hold of her sister's hand and set off across the grass towards the white-owned farm where Nono worked.

It was a long walk. Dineo became tired and Naledi picked her up and carried her on her back. They walked across the veld, where the villagers let their *cattle graze*, and then up to the road between the *wire fences* of the farms owned by white people. *Pipes* carrying water ran alongside rows of fresh, green plants. Not like the ones on their land.

pipe

So many thoughts were running through her mind. How could Chief Sekete have reached an agreement with these white people? When he had first heard of the plans for *removal*, why hadn't he spoken of them at the **kgotla**,* the place where all village matters were

---

slope, a piece of rising or falling ground; an area of land that is part of a mountain
veld [**velt**], (in South Africa) flat open land with grass and no trees
graze, to eat growing grass
removal, the process of removing something or somebody
*traditional meeting

wire fence

grass

cattle = several cows

discussed? The land had belonged to the Sekete family for over seventy-five years, from before the time when the law said only whites could buy land. Everyone knew the story of how Chief Sekete's grandfather had bought the farm from an Englishman who had decided that 5 farming here wasn't for him. There was not enough rain, not like across the sea from where he had come. Chief Sekete's grandfather had called this place Bophelong, 'the place where we get life'. They would *survive*, like their fathers before them, in the land 10

survive, to continue to live or exist even in very difficult times

where there was not enough water.

Naledi knew this story. She was often a guest in Chief Sekete's house, as the chief's daughter Poleng was her closest friend. The chief had always seemed especially kind to her, as her own father was dead. But what could she think now? Was it possible that Poleng too had known about the removal and had not said anything? The thought troubled her.

The news she carried would be a terrible shock to their grandmother, which was why Naledi wanted to tell her herself. Nono looked after them while their mother worked far off in the city for a white family. The law would not let Mma keep her children with her. And how would Mma take the news? She was so far away, what could she do?

Like most of the older people around, Nono had not been able to find any paid work. Then, by chance, a friend who had worked in the garden at a white farm became too ill to continue and she had sent Nono in her place. At first the white woman at the farmhouse had said Nono looked too old, but as the work was mainly *weeding* she would try her out.

"I have to be careful whom I have near the house these days. I suppose I can trust someone older like you," she had added.

The pay was only five **rand*** per week. On rare occasions Nono was given a few oranges or *vegetables* when the farm produced more than was needed. Somehow

---

weed, to take out wild plants from the ground especially in a garden or in a field

*the unit of money in the Republic of South Africa; 100 cents

vegetable ['vedʒtəbl], a plant or part of a plant eaten as food

they managed with their small incomes. Why did this new *threat* have to come to them now?

Yet terrible things were happening to other people all the time. She had learned so much through her friendship with Grace Mbatha, the young woman from Soweto* who had helped her and Tiro when they had been looking for their mother in Jo'burg* when Dineo was ill. Ever since then, they had been writing to each other. There were always threats where Grace lived in Soweto, near Jo'burg, and recently Naledi had begun to worry that her friend might be in trouble herself. She had not heard from her for some time. Grace's letters often carried news of *protests* against schools, rents, taxes, of stonings, burnings, of attacks by police, shootings and *arrests*. Grace wrote about these things in a sort of *code*.

Reading Grace's letters usually left Naledi feeling angry and upset. Here in Bophelong she was so far away and quite unable to help. Yet now, all of a sudden, they too were in danger... and she was unprepared.

Naledo and Dineo finally reached the long drive to the farm. On either side there was a variety of trees and

threat [θret], the possibility of trouble or danger; an expression to harm somebody if they do not do as one wishes
*Southwest *Township*, (a town or part of a town where black people lived) at that time a "black" area of Johannesburg
*Johannesburg
protest ['prəʊtest], a statement or an action to show that one is against something
arrest, to take and keep somebody in prison (that is a place where a person is locked up if he has done a crime) with the authority of the law
code, a system of words, letters or numbers used to send messages or information that should be understood only by the person who receives them

11

plants. Naledo usually looked at all the flowers and fruits, but today she saw only a picture of a great *lorry* driving up to their house and police forcing them onto it. To make it worse, in her picture, the father of her
5 friend Poleng was standing by, watching.

Chapter 3

Turning the corner of the drive near the farmhouse, Naledi examined the garden at the front of the long white house. Nono was nowhere to be seen. As Nale-
10 di was walking around the side of the house, the dogs suddenly came running towards her, *barking* wildly. A woman working outside the kitchen looked up. She shouted to the dogs and pointed to where Nono was working. Across the thick, green grass and close to the blue swimming pool, Nono was on all fours, weeding
15 the *lawn*. As soon as Dineo saw her, she ran to her *granny*, calling, "Nono! Nono!"

"Why have you come? Why are you not in school?" Nono's face was worried. Naledi helped her get up. "It's something bad at home, Nono! A man is painting
20 numbers on all the doors and two white men are there. They say we all have to go. They say lorries are coming soon."

"What?"

"We can all refuse, Nono! What can they..."

---

lorry, a large, strong motor car for transporting goods, soldiers, etc.
bark, (of dogs) to give a bark (or barks), that is a short, sharp sound
lawn, area of grass in a garden
granny, grandmother

She stopped suddenly. The 'Missus'* was approaching.

"What's going on here, Martha?" asked a young white woman. "Why aren't you in school today?" she turned to Naledi.

"I had to bring my grandmother some news. It's bad news... Missus." She hated using that word. Most white people expected that a black person should say it to show their respect for them. She could get into a lot of trouble if she did not say it.

"What is it then?"

Nono answered with her eyes turned away.

"The child says someone is putting numbers on our houses, Missus. They say we have to go somewhere else."

"But didn't you know that?" the white woman asked. Nono *shook her head.*

"Well, I don't think you should worry too much, Martha. I'm sure it'll work out well in the end. It was planned a long time ago that all you black people should go to live together in your own place. You know, your own *homeland* just for yourselves. You're lucky it's not so far from here, and they say there'll be buses. Maybe just a one- or two-hour ride, so you can still come here to work each day. Then at night you can go back to your own home."

Nono and Naledi were quite silent. Only Dineo moved.

---

*title of respect for a white woman
shake one's head, to move the head from side to side to say 'no'
homeland, an area where black people were made to live

13

"Look, you don't have to worry! I'm prepared to wait for a couple of weeks for you. Then if you travel here on the bus, you can still have your job."

Very softly, Nono replied, "Yes, Missus."

5 "Listen, if the child helps you a bit now, I'll let you go early today. Just finish weeding this section of the lawn."

"Thank you, Missus," Nono answered softly. Only Naledi heard the pain in her voice.

****

10 It was mid-afternoon, when they reached the village. Usually it would be fairly quiet at this time, but today people stood in twos and threes outside their houses. The large white numbers shone brightly on the brown doors.

15 As they approached a group of women, a voice called out.

"Mma! How is it with you?"

Without waiting for a reply, their *relative* Mma Kau hurried over to help support Nono for the rest of the
20 *journey* home. Once inside, Nono was gently lifted onto the bed.

As Naledi was beginning to cook, Tiro came running into the house.

"It's also Boomdal! They're also going to move
25 Boomdal! They put numbers there too! Your friend Taolo just told me."

Boomdal was where they went to school. It was a

relative, a person in the same family as oneself
journey ['dʒɜːnɪ], the act of travelling from one place to another

township for black people near the white town.

"Tell us what the chief said to Mma Tshadi," Nono said from the bed. "Your sister told me you went to hear them."

Everyone knew that Mma Tshadi and the chief 5 didn't get along, though they were related. Mma Tshadi was certainly the most outspoken member of the village, and she often commented on the amount of alcohol the chief drank. She ran a small shop from her house. The other shops were an hour's walk away in 10 Boomdal.

"When we got to the chief's house," Tiro began, "Mma Sekete said her husband was still asleep. You should have seen Mma Tshadi's face! So Mma Sekete said she would get him up. When he came to the door, 15 he looked very angry at being woken up. But after Mma Tshadi finished with him, he looked sick. He didn't say anything, only that he will hold a kgotla later this afternoon."

"Did you see Poleng?" Naledi asked quietly. 20

Tiro shook his head.

Chapter 4

The sky that had been so clear and blue early that morning was grey as Naledi and Tiro arrived at the small church hall late in the afternoon. Word had been sent around by the chief that this unexpected 25 kgotla would take place here.

The hall was already full of people. The air in the room was hot and people were speaking in angry, worried voices. Naledi saw Poleng, standing at the back,

15

almost out of sight. What would she say to her when they met?

People moved aside to make way for Chief Sekete and two of his brothers. They lived with their families near the city of Pretoria and only returned to the family home at Bophelong at Christmas and on special occasions. Chief Sekete must have told them to come quickly for this special kgotla.

The chief moved forward. "My people, this is a difficult time for us. As you know, sometimes the weather changes and we are forced to change our plans about how we shall plant or how we shall build. In the beginning we *complain*, but then sometimes we find that everything has worked out well. It isn't easy to see ahead..."

He *paused*, but before he could continue, Mma Tshadi stood up.

"None of us can say what the weather will be. Tonight we have not come to discuss the plans of the weather but the plans of the whites. Just tell us about these plans."

An *elderly* man stood up. It was Rra* Rampou.

"Pardon me if I speak out of turn, but I am very worried. I have lived in this place since I was born. My father rented from your father and now they both rest under the earth in this place. This is where my body must rest when my time comes. So what we want to know is this: What do the numbers mean?"

As voices rose again, the chief put up his hand.

complain, to say that one is unhappy or not satisfied
pause [pɔːz], to stop talking or doing something for a while
elderly, (of people) rather old
*Mr; Sir; father

"I hadn't finished speaking when Mma Tshadi *inter-rupted*. I was telling you that sometimes we have to change our plans. That is happening to us now. We are being asked to go and live in our own homeland."

"This land, right here, is our home! What 'home- land' are you talking about?" This time Mma Tshadi did not even wait for the chief to pause before asking her question.

"I am talking about Bophuthatswana - the place for people who speak Tswana."

"What about those who speak other languages?" A deep voice came from the back.

"They will be able to go to their own homelands."

"What 'homelands' are these you talk about? People are living in peace together in their own homes right here, as did their fathers and mothers before them, even their grandparents. Why should they want another home?"

"Listen to reason, my people! We know these things have already been decided by the highest councils in the land by those with power. Surely it is better for us to accept - "

"Accept?" The deep voice sounded again from the back. "**You** wish to accept, but did you ask the opinion of anyone here?"

By now everyone was turning around to look at the speaker. Naledi saw that it was Taolo's father, Saul Dikobe. Next to him was Taolo, the boy who within the twelve months since he arrived had become the most outspoken student in their school. He was in the class

interrupt, to stop somebody speaking or doing something by speaking oneself or disturbing in some other way

above Naledi. This was the first time Taolo's father had come to a kgotla, because the government had '*banned*' him. It was well known that he was not allowed to talk to more than two people, otherwise the police would put him back in prison. Clearly he was taking a big risk this evening by coming to the meeting.

Naledi had heard Taolo explain that his father had already spent ten years in prison for helping workers in their factories. The family had then lived in Soweto. But as soon as his father came out of prison, the authorities had sent him to this village far away. Just before he had arrived, the white *magistrate* had come to tell the villagers how they would find themselves in trouble if they had anything to do with Saul Dikobe. The message had had its effect. People had kept clear of the Dikobe house. Mma Dikobe had a friendly smile and worked in the hospital. Although Taolo was popular in school, no one visited him at home. In fact, the only regular visitors to the house were policemen coming to check on Saul Dikobe, usually at night.

Now Saul Dikobe's deep voice kept coming from the back. Chief Sekete held up his hand for silence and pointed straight at Saul Dikobe. "You are a troublemaker, an *agitator*! You should not be here! If my people listen to you, things will go badly for them. Leave them alone!"

"Can a chief not trust his people to hear different voices? Are they children who must listen only to the

ban, to forbid somebody to do something (especially officially)
magistrate ['mædʒɪstreɪt], an official who acts as a judge in the lowest courts
agitator ['ædʒɪteɪtə], a person who encourages others to protest; to agitate, to demand something publicly or take part in a demonstration

words of their parents?"

Before Chief Sekete could reply, one of his brothers at the table interrupted. "Let us not argue. This is a hard time for us all, so let my brother explain what he knows of this removal." 5

The rain outside beat down on the *roof* as Chief Sekete began again: he and his brothers, being the landowners, had known for a few months about the plans for the removal. However, they hadn't wanted to worry anyone else until the matter was fully settled. 10 The magistrate had explained to them that all the villagers who were paying rent were *'squatters'* according to the law, so they had no right to stay, even if their parents had lived here before them. The chief had been taken to see where the village would be moved. Part of 15 it had once been an area of white farms. The man from 'Affairs' had promised that the government would build houses for all the villagers before the removal.

A deep, dry laugh broke out from the back. It was Saul Dikobe again. "Do you know what they call 'a 20 house'? Which sort did they tell you about? The ones made with a roof where you can cook like meat when it's hot and turn to ice when it's cold? Or the tomato box made from wood, which lets in the wind? My friends, let us ask our chief if he is going to be living in 25 such a 'house'."

Chief Sekete rested his hand on the table. People were waiting for his reply. No... his house would be a little different. Because his family were landowners,

---

roof, a structure covering or forming the top of a building
squatter, a person who settles on land, especially public or new land, without title or right

they were to be given houses that had previously been occupied by white families.

Many questions were now put forward. What about their *crops* already growing in the fields? What would they have to eat for the rest of the year if they had to leave these behind? Why were they called 'squatters'? What land would they have for planting? Where would they find work? Were there schools? Was there a hospital? Life was hard here, but at least they somehow kept alive. They had heard how things were in a place now called 'Bop'. A few people had got rich there, but if you were poor, then it was only a place for dying.

As the questions and comments grew louder, Chief Sekete's brothers began to *whisper* to each other. Raising his voice, the chief announced that these were matters that should rather be put to someone from the 'Affairs' department. He would see if a meeting could be arranged, but for now, the kgotla was over. With that, almost pushing the chief between them, his brothers made their way through the crowd to the door.

The yard outside the church hall filled with bodies and voices in the dark. In the *crowd* Naledi held on to Tiro's shoulder.

"Naledi?"

She looked up through the rain, straight into the wet face of her friend Poleng.

"Let me talk to you, please!" Poleng said. "I didn't know, Naledi! Truly I didn't know!"

crop, plants growing in the fields
whisper ['wɪspə], to say something quietly so that only the people closest to one can hear
crowd [kraʊd], a large number of people gathered together

"When did you find out?"

"Today. Just like you. When Mma Tshadi came to our house. I heard what was going on. My father wouldn't let me go to school after that."

"What did your father tell you?" asked Naledi. 5

"He said it's better for us to move, because we can never win against the government."

Poleng paused, as if what she had to say next was difficult. "He also said... our family will have a nice house to live in... and he might send me... away to school." 10

"To *boarding school*? Where will he get the money?"

Poleng began to cry. "I don't know... That's what he said... and on the way here, no one would talk to me. They just gave me bad looks... "

Poor Poleng, thought Naledi. She was upset by what 15 her father had done. It wasn't her fault.

Naledi was about to put her arm around Poleng when Chief Sekete called her to come home.

Chapter 5

Poleng did not appear for the walk to school the next day. Naledi waited a short while for her near Mma 20 Tshadi's, but when she didn't arrive, she realized that her father must be keeping her away again. Was he expecting trouble?

Not all the children from Bophelong went to school. Only those whose parents could *afford* to send them. 25

---

boarding school, a school where some or all of the pupils live during the term

afford, to have enough money for a particular purpose

They walked to Boomdal each morning in small groups and pairs.

The *primary school* began earlier than the high school in order to fit in two sessions with different pupils, so Tiro had already gone. As Naledi set off without Poleng, she kept a lookout for Taolo Dikobe. Sometimes he would join them. She liked him. He did not seem to be afraid to say what he thought, even to the headmaster. Mr Molaba was not used to such behaviour, and Taolo had soon received a number of beatings. Yet each time he became more angry and determined. His mother was called to the school. Word went around that Mrs Dikobe had stood up for her son, telling Mr Molaba that she and his father had always told their son to be *honest* and truthful. His father had gone to prison for ten years because of what he believed. The headmaster was shocked. No one had talked to him like that before. According to Taolo, Mr Molaba had ended the interview by telling his mother, "I shall give him one last chance. But you had better talk some sense into him if he wants to continue here."

Naledi had the feeling that Taolo liked her too, although the only time they really talked to each other was on their way to and from school. When he found out that she had been to Soweto and was writing to a friend in the middle of all the protest there, he had begun to speak openly about some of his feelings. It was clear that he missed his old home in Soweto. Yes, he and his friends had felt that death could be around the

primary school, a school for children between 5 and 11 years old
honest ['ɒnɪst], (of a person) telling the truth

22

corner. There were *informers*, *spies* and armed police almost everywhere. But Taolo and his friends were to be part of a great *revolt* against *apartheid*.

After his father had been *released* from prison, he had not even been allowed one night in their Soweto 5 home. The police had taken him immediately to Bophelong. Because of the banning order, his father could not work. *Fortunately* Mrs Dikobe had managed to get a job in the small country hospital. So the family was at last together in this far away village after 10 eleven years *apart*.

Taolo was not happy. He very much wanted to be back with all his friends in the middle of the action in Soweto, but he also wanted to be with his father. He had so few memories of being with him at all before 15 the age of five, when they had been parted. With all his political work, Saul Dikobe had never had much time for his family.

Walking by herself up the muddy track of the village, Naledi thought about the kgotla and how Saul 20 Dikobe had talked to the chief. What would the government do if someone like Taolo's father were the chief and he refused to go along with them?

informer, a person who informs the police about other people
spy, here, a person who watches and reports on what others do, where they go etc and tells the police; *to spy*, to be a spy
revolt, a fight of a group of people against authority or those in power
apartheid [ə'pɑːteɪt], (formerly in South Africa) a political system which placed power in the hands of white South Africans and refused political and social rights to people of other races; setting the whites apart.
release, to allow a person to be set free; the action of releasing somebody
fortunate, lucky
apart, that is separated from each other

23

"Naledi!"

She stopped and turned. It was Taolo running up the track.

"Where's your friend? Is she hiding her face again today?"

"She can't help what her father does. She's upset."

"So, she's got a problem. We all have. First they throw our family out of Soweto and now they want to throw everyone out of here."

"So what can we do?"

"Fight back, of course. My father says that in a few places the people are still on their land, although they were told to leave long ago."

"But if we refuse, they'll come with dogs and guns - and what do we have to fight back with?"

"Look, sis, in Soweto children have been *resisting* with just their hands and stones against trucks, *tanks* with fully armed police and soldiers. Okay, so they keep killing us, but they still can't break us. Even more people are on our side now. Parents see what the police are doing to their children and they also join in the struggle. We're getting stronger all the time."

Naledi didn't reply. A picture came to her mind. Their homes *surrounded* by soldiers and tanks...

"There's not just one way of fighting," Taolo continued as if reading her mind. "We can check the law. Maybe we'll find something there that we can use. They always shout to the world about 'law and order'! Everything - even their killing - is done by the law!"

---

resist, to offer opposition; to refuse to agree
surround, to be all round something or somebody

tank

As Taolo spoke and Naledi listened - about newspapers, campaigns and getting others to support them - it all began to seem possible. Maybe they could, one way or another, stop the government's plan! The first, the most important thing was to be well organized. In Boomdal people had formed their own *Residents'* Association some time ago. Taolo said that the villagers of Bophelong should have followed their example. Instead, they had continued to put all their trust in one person, who was being paid by white authorities - Chief Sekete.

Naledi knew, inside herself, that what Taolo was saying about her friend's father was true.

"We must do the same as Boomdal and join with them!" he continued, looking directly at Naledi. "What do you say, sis?"

She turned her face to him and said sharply, "All right! So how do we start?"

---

resident ['rezɪdənt], a person who lives in a place

Chapter 6

As they walked into the school grounds, there was no time to talk to other students. The classes were lining up in front of the single-storey grey building. Mr Molaba was standing on the steps overseeing the operation
5 as if he were a military officer. A large man with a broad face and small eyes, he had deep lines that seemed to pull at his mouth.

"I have an announcement to make. You all know by now that you and your families are due to move from
10 here in the very near future. I have not received information about the school you will be able to attend in the homeland, but I should like to *warn* all of you to *behave* well in your last few weeks at this school. It may even be that you and I will meet again in your next
15 school..."

Mr Molaba paused, looking down at lines of faces.

"In any event, all school records will be kept up to date until your very last day here, before they are sent on." Shouting the number of each class in turn, he
20 watched with attention as the students marched away.

In the lesson that followed with Mr Gwala, Naledi found it difficult to concentrate. She was not the only one. There were so many important questions to be answered. Why did Mr Molaba make that remark
25 about being in their next school? Was he to be its head-

---

warn, to inform somebody of a possible danger or something unpleasant that is likely to happen, before it happens, so that they can try to avoid it
behave [bɪ'heɪv], to act in a correct way with good manners

26

master? Naledi felt sure that he knew more than he had said.

"What is it, Naledi? You don't seem to be working hard today," her teacher said.

As Naledi stood up wondering what to say, an idea went through her mind. Mr Gwala was easier to talk to than most of the teachers.

"Sir," she began, "where will you go if they force Tswanas into the place they say is our 'homeland'?"

The class was completely silent, all eyes on the teacher. Everyone knew that although he spoke Tswana, Mr Gwala's first language was Zulu.

"Well, Naledi... since you ask, I have to tell you that I don't know. This business is as much a shock to me as it must be to all of you. I know that non-Tswanas aren't welcome in Bop, so I wouldn't be able to teach there for sure. If we are forced from here, the only place I could get a teaching job would be far away in KwaZulu."

"Do you want to go there, sir?" asked the boy next to Naledi.

"I haven't been there since my grandparents died when I was a child. My parents made their home here in the Transvaal," the teacher replied quietly.

For a few seconds no one said a word. It would be too personal to ask Mr Gwala to explain. Then a girl put up a hand.

"What is it, Miriam?"

"Sir, my mother speaks Tswana but my father's first language is Sotho. They have been living here together in Boomdal for twenty years. What will happen to them now?"

"I really don't know, Miriam."

"Is anything wrong, Mr Gwala?" Mr Molaba was at

the door. Before Miriam could sit down, the headmaster asked her to bring up her work. She walked slowly forward, book in hand. Mr Molaba looked at the almost empty page.

5 "Is this all you have done this morning? You are in Standard Seven and you cannot do long *multiplications*? I think you had better present yourself outside my office every breaktime this week so that you can learn. Don't you agree, Mr Gwala?"

10 He didn't wait for Mr Gwala to reply. "If there are any others who do not complete the work that has been set, you can see them at breaktime yourself... can you not, Mr Gwala?"

Naledi felt sorry for their teacher. How she hated Mr
15 Molaba and all those like him who enjoyed *crushing* others. But there was no time for *emotion*. Mr Gwala was telling the class that they had five minutes to finish all the problems. They all turned to their books. Then with surprise and *relief* they saw that Mr Gwala
20 was writing the answers into their correct spaces on the board!

"Hurry up!" was all he said.

****

At the back of the building furthest from the headmaster's office, Naledi found a crowd of students
25 already around Taolo. His voice was angry. "They take

---

multiplication, the action or process of multiplying, this is to add a number to itself a particular number of times: 2 multiplied by 4 is 8
crush, here, to press or to damage completely
emotion, a strong feeling
relief, a feeling when worry or pain has been removed

six pieces of land and put some 'President' in charge. Then they say, 'These pieces aren't South Africa anymore. From now on we say they are Bophuthatswana, and any Tswanas we don't want, we send them there.' They take a few more pieces somewhere else and say, '- These are KwaZulu and they'll do for the Zulus... And the Xhosas can have these pieces over here,' and so on. They want to force us back to the days of our great-grandfathers, pushing us here and there, keeping us apart so they can control us! Hell man, the **whole** of South Africa belongs to us - all of us! Why shouldn't we be free to make our home wherever we choose, live with whomever we want? I ask you, what good is there in that place they call our 'homeland'?"

"But some people say it's better there in Bop, that blacks are at least free to get to the top instead of always being under some white boss."

It was one of the older Boomdal students who spoke.

"What do you mean 'free'? This chief they made 'President' must still say, 'Yes, sir, no, sir,' to big white chief Botha*. Look, it's Botha who pays his salary! I tell you the only 'freedom' in Bop is for the 'President' and his friends to make money for themselves and - "

"It's true!" a girl said. "My father's sister was forced to Bop. All her life she had lived in Potchefstroom. Then one day the police came, broke the houses, pushed everyone onto trucks and cleared the whole place. They took her to Rooigrond - do you know what Rooigrond is? It's... it's just dry red earth, no fields, no grass.

---

*Pieter Willem Botha, South African politician, Prime Minister 1978-84, President 1984-89

29

At her home my *aunt* had land and animals. But the *cows* died on the trucks and the police forced her to leave the *pigs*. Maybe the whites took them, but she didn't get any money. There's nothing at Rooigrond.
5 People are *starving* there now. Is that 'freedom'?"

cow   pig

As the girl spoke, Naledi felt that it was no good listening to these terrible stories. They had to **do** something.

"We must refuse to go!" she shouted. "All of us must
10 refuse!"

With shouts of agreement coming from all sides, Taolo started again. "In Soweto the students got their parents to take action. In Boomdal you have a committee, but in Bophelong there's -"
15 "SO!"

Without warning, Mr Molaba came marching between them. "So! We have our young agitator at work. Your mother won't be able to get you out of this

---

aunt, the sister of one's father or mother or the wife of one's uncle
starve, to suffer or die from lack of food

30

one so easily. It'll be the police she'll be seeing next, not me!"

Taolo remained silent, but returned Mr Molaba's stare until the headmaster turned his head away, letting his eyes move across the whole group.

"I will not have politics discussed in my school! I have told you before and I repeat it. I will not have anyone bring politics into these grounds, especially when that person has a known troublemaker for a father!"

"We are only talking about our own lives! You shouldn't stop us." Naledi was taken by surprise to hear her own voice.

"'Shouldn't'? You, a pupil in my school, think you can tell me what I 'shouldn't' do? I see that Dikobe the young agitator has had some success already. Well, we shall see how much you want to follow in his footsteps when I'm finished. Both of you go to my office. As for the rest, get to your classes immediately and stop playing at being grown-ups. You are playing with fire!"

Chapter 7

For a long time afterwards Naledi couldn't think about what followed in the headmaster's office without reliving the terrible *humiliation*. She felt that she could never forget the shock and *anger* inside her when Mr Molaba pulled out his thin *cane*, put a chair into the middle

humiliation [hjuː,mɪlɪˈeɪʃən], the act of making somebody feel low and worthless
anger, the state of being angry
cane, see picture, page 32

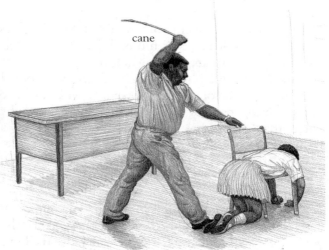

cane

Naledi is bending over the chair

of the room and pointed to Naledi to *bend* over it.

"You won't change anything by beating her! In Soweto students are *boycotting* their schools to stop the beatings!" Taolo cried.

5   "You are not in Soweto here! Now you can see the result of your work in agitating students in my school."

He opened the door and told Miriam, who was waiting outside, to call the four biggest boys in the top class to come immediately. On presenting themselves, they 10 were ordered to take hold of Taolo's arms.

"Let's all watch a big grown man beat up a fifteen-

---

boycott, to refuse to take part in something or to have social contact or do business with a person, company, country, etc, as a way of protesting about something

year-old girl just because he doesn't like what she says!" Taolo cried.

The cane cut through the air and hit Naledi's body causing terrible pain. She forced back the *tears*... three... four... oh God... five... six... wasn't that it?... oh 5 help me... seven, eight, nine, ten...

Mr Molaba ordered her to pull herself up and stand properly. Her legs could hardly carry her.

"Now let that be a lesson to you and to everyone else in this school. I hope you have learned what comes of 10 listening to troublemakers. Do you understand me?"

Naledi was aware that the headmaster was waiting for her to answer him, but she kept silent. She was not going to talk against Taolo now or ever. The Dikobes were right. You had to struggle. 15

"You have until tomorrow morning to come with your reply to me, otherwise you risk being *expelled* from the school like that '*hero*' of yours." Mr Molaba turned to Taolo.

"I am expelling you from this school. I shall give you 20 a letter for your parents and my decision is final. There's no point in your mother coming to see me again. I shall be informing the Department and the *Inspector* immediately."

Taolo said nothing and just stared straight ahead of 25 him. The other four students looked even more ill at ease than before.

---

tear [tɪə], a drop of water that comes from the eye when one cries
expel, to force somebody to leave school
hero, a person that one looks up to because of his good qualities
inspector, an official who visits the schools to see that the rules are obeyed

Once Naledi was outside the office, Miriam was there and took her arm, helping her to the tap. She drank a few mouthfuls. The water on her face gave her some relief for a few seconds from the sharp pain in her body. Then Miriam led her to the back of one of the buildings, where she could rest without being seen from the classrooms.

"We can wait here until you feel okay," Miriam spoke softly.

"Don't you... have to stay... outside his office?"

"I don't care anymore. I could hear everything inside! You stood up to him, so why shouldn't I? Anyway, what's the point?... There'll be no school for me soon." If they were moved and Boomdal was *destroyed*, Miriam said, their father would lose his job and they'd have no money. Non-Tswanas were not welcome in Bop and her father was Sotho, so how would they manage? Even if a school accepted her and her sisters and brothers because their mother was a Tswana speaker, the family would not be able to afford schooling anymore.

"But we don't have to give in!" Naledi said. "If we learn to stand together, we can fight them! Look, after school we'll talk with Taolo. Molaba can't stop us doing that."

Naledi began to walk in the direction of her classroom. "I'll be alright now." She lifted her head. She would not let Mr Molaba have the pleasure of seeing her in pain.

---

destroy, to damage something so badly that it no longer exists, works, etc

34

Chapter 8

As students crowded out through the gates after the lessons, Naledi found arms on her shoulders and words of sympathy coming from all sides. Everyone knew what had happened. The issue was not finished. Mr Molaba had said he would give her until the next day 5 to promise to *obey* his rules, or be expelled herself. He didn't seem to care about the high quality of her schoolwork. Although she was pleased with some of the remarks being made now, she was feeling cold inside. 10

"We shouldn't let him get away with it! He thinks he can just expel someone... as easy as that. We should do something to make him take Taolo back!"

"He won't listen, even if we just want to speak to him." 15

"... and the Inspector will back him up."

"Why don't we boycott? Like in Soweto!"

"What can that do? They already want to shut the school so they can move us."

Naledi walked slowly, wondering whether Taolo had 20 already taken his letter of *expulsion* to his mother at the hospital and whether he would come back past the school. It was *silly* of course, she knew.

Joining the small group of students on the path for Bophelong, Naledi missed Poleng. Perhaps Chief 25 Sekete would not let her return to school at all. Naledi spoke very little on the way home, too many thoughts

---

obey, to do what one is told
expulsion, the act of expelling
silly, not showing thought or understanding

were going through her head. What was she to answer Mr Molaba? If she were expelled, what would be the effect on Nono? She had never seen her grandmother as *weak* and ill as this before. Another shock might be too much for her. Yet how was Nono going to survive being forced out of her own home? Somehow they **had** to stop the removal. She must see Taolo and his father. The way he had spoken at the meeting showed he understood exactly what they were up against.

Naledi was so deep in thought that although she was aware of the sound of a car, she didn't look up at it until it was practically on them. It was travelling fast, coming from the direction of Bophelong. Someone took hold of her arm, pulling her aside from the road. She looked up just in time to see the blue car from the day before and, to her shock, Poleng's face looking *anxiously* out from the back window. Among the heads in the car she saw Poleng's father and mother.

"Where are they off to in such a hurry?" asked the older Sadire boy, David, who had pulled her aside from the road.

"I don't know... but look there"!

They could now see the Sekete house and a small crowd gathering in front of it. Suddenly she saw her brother come out of the crowd.

"What's happening?" Naledi asked when she reached him.

"The white men came to take the chief away. They took cases with them."

---

weak, not strong
anxious ['æŋʃəs], feeling nervous and worried

36

Mma Tshadi's strong voice took over. "I will tell you young people from the high school something else so you can tell it to those who are not here. Our chief has *deserted* us. He is *frightened*. So he needs the white man to protect him. That is why he asked the white man to take him and his family away. He will go to the big house he has been promised in our 'homeland'. But first, I am sure they will build a great fence around his new house. Is that not strange? A chief should protect his people. But now he wants protection from them!" 10

Apart from the children, the crowd was made up largely of older women and men. Naledi did not immediately notice the newcomer standing in the background. Only when David Sadire cried, "Jerry," did Naledi recognize him as the son Mma Kau had been 15 anxiously waiting to return from his first contract on the gold *mines*. But in one year something in his manner had changed. Although David and Jerry were very different, as boys they had been so close. Jerry had unexpectedly dropped out of school to sign up for Ego- 20 li, the city of gold where young men were always needed to go down into the mines. Now, as Naledi watched them, Jerry Kau gave only half his attention to his former friend. He was listening to what the old people were saying. Then Mma Tshadi turned to Naledi. 25

"Tell that young friend of yours, Dikobe's son, to come and see me. All the words his father spoke last night were true. Perhaps he can advise us now."

"Yes, Mma, I'll ask him to come to you tonight."

---

desert [dɪ'zɜːt], to leave somebody without help or support
frighten, to make somebody afraid
gold *mine*, a place under ground from where gold is taken out

It was a relief. At last something was beginning to happen. Naledi called Tiro.

"Let's go! We must see how Nono is."

Chapter 9

Nono was lying on the bed, quite still. Mma Kau was sitting on a nearby chair with Dineo. Standing by the bed, Naledi gently held her grandmother's hand. Nono's eyes slowly opened, looked at Naledi and then closed again.

Going outside with Mma Kau, Naledi said, "I'll go to Mma Dikobe. Perhaps she can help."

Banning order or no banning order, she would go to the forbidden house. Mma Dikobe was a *nurse*. She had always looked friendly and surely would not refuse to help. Anyway, she had promised Mma Tshadi to get a message to Taolo.

"I see your son has returned, Mma. You must be very happy to have him back," Naledi added before leaving.

"Yes," Mma Kau said with a smile. "He went away a boy but he has come back a man."

****

Houses in Bophelong were built well apart, and the authorities had placed the Dikobes in one far away from the others at the western end of the village.

There was no sign of anyone outside the house and the door was closed, although one of the windows was slightly open. Before Naledi reached the house the door was opened and Taolo stepped out.

"I can't ask you in, so we'll have to talk here. Three makes a banned gathering, you know!"

nurse, a person trained to help a doctor to look after sick or injured people

"You mean they watch all the time?" Naledi was shocked.

"You don't know when they're watching. That's their game - you can never be sure."

5 "But I'm not coming to see your father. I want to see your mother and you."

"So tell that to the police and see if they believe you!"

While they were speaking, Taolo looked around the
10 area. The only other house in sight was Rra Thopi's.

"Look... I'm very sorry about what happened to you today. But I'm glad you stood up to Mr Molaba. Now at least you understand a little more what to expect when you start to resist those with power."

15 "I came to ask if your mother will come to see my grandmother. She's very ill... ever since she heard the news. My other message is for you from Mma Tshadi. She wants you to visit her right away. Chief Sekete has packed his cases and gone with his family. Mma Tsha-
20 di thinks your father can help."

Taolo smiled. "So your chief has finally shown himself up! Mma and I came straight from the hospital. We didn't see or hear anything. But I'm sorry about your grandmother. I'll call my mother for you right away."

25 Naledi looked around her while she waited, wondering from where the police could spy.

Soon Mma Dikobe came out and *greeted* Naledi. "Taolo has told me about you. I'm pleased you came. Give me a minute and I'll put a few things in my bag I

---

greet, to give a sign or word of welcome or pleasure when meeting somebody or receiving a guest

might need for your grandmother."

Taolo walked with Naledi and his mother through the village until they came to the church. Then he took another path to Mma Tshadi's.

Mma Dikobe sat down next to Nono and spoke soft- 5
ly, saying why she had come. She took Nono's temperature and carefully checked her blood pressure which was very high. Together Mma Dikobe and Mma Kau washed Nono and changed her clothes.

"It helps to feel a little fresher," Mma Dikobe said. 10
"You must not worry. Just lie here and have plenty of rest to get your strength back. I have some *tablets* to help you and something for you to drink. Even if you don't feel like eating, you must still drink."

Producing a small bottle and a couple of tablets from 15
her bag, Mma Dikobe turned to Naledi. "You must make sure that she keeps drinking and that she takes these tablets."

It was getting dark. She promised to call in and see Nono the following day. Then Mma Kau left. She had 20
prepared them some food. Dineo had already eaten and was ready to go to sleep.

Naledi lit the lamp and sat down with Tiro to eat. It was only when the lamp was out, and they had settled down onto their *mats* in the small room at the side, 25
that Tiro asked Naledi what had happened. There was no door between them and the main room, so he kept his voice to a low whisper. He had heard talk of Naledi's beating when he had gone to collect the evening's water at the village tap. 30

tablet ['tæblət], a small amount of medicine in a hard form
mat, a piece of material used to cover a part of the floor

41

"Why didn't you tell me?" Tiro asked.

"There wasn't time. We were at the Chief's place and then I had to get Mma Dikobe."

"Then tell me now."

5   Naledi told him what had happened and when she had finished, Tiro was very upset.

"I'd like to get that headmaster and give him a beating like he gave you!" he whispered angrily. He turned to face the wall. Naledi put her hand on his arm but he
10 pulled it away.

Chapter 10

Naledi must have been sleeping lightly, because the sound of footsteps running past the house woke her. She would probably have gone back to sleep if she had not noticed a strange light through the thin *curtains*.
15 Normally the village was completely quiet and very dark unless the moon was up. But lifting the curtain, Naledi was shocked to see huge *flames* in the black sky over in the direction of Poleng's house. She woke Tiro and the two of them stared out in silence. Then they
20 saw a couple of dark figures in the neighbouring yard.

"I want to go out and see what's happening," Tiro whispered.

"No. If the police come, there'll be trouble."

"Who did it? What do you think?"

25   Naledi gave no reply. She thought about Poleng and

curtain ['kɜːtən], a piece of material hung to cover a window. Usually it can be pulled from side to side
flame, a hot quantity of burning gas that comes from something on fire with a bright light

42

was glad that she was gone. Perhaps the chief had known this might happen. But who would actually do this? It couldn't possibly be Taolo, could it? She said nothing to Tiro.

****

With the sky beginning to lighten, Naledi took Nono 5 a glass of water and gave her a couple more of Mma Dikobe's tablets. Dineo was still sleeping as her sister and brother went outside quietly. It was usual for them to leave early to collect the day's water from the village tap. But today instead of going towards the tap near 10 the church, they ran in between the mud walls and wire fences of neighbouring yards in the direction of the chief's house.

Others were already there, staring at blackened and smoking walls. A voice in the gathering mentioned 15 the word 'police'. Yes, the police would soon be here, asking questions. There was already another question she had not yet decided how to answer, and Mr Mola- ba was expecting a reply today. Should she tell him she was sorry, which she wasn't, or risk being expelled? 20

She needed to talk to someone. Suddenly Naledi knew who it was. Mma Dikobe, who seemed so calm yet determined. She had promised to call in on Nono. Naledi decided she would stay at home with Nono today. She would take a message to the farm to say that 25 Nono was ill. Let Mr Molaba wait!

While they were waiting to fill their *buckets* at the

| *bucket*, see picture, page 5

tap, the police arrived. A loud noise was heard in the distance and everybody looked through the early light towards the track from town. Soon they saw a dark *van* slowing down near the chief's house and coming to a
5 stop by the church. A white officer stepped down from the front as a group of black police jumped out from the doors at the back. The van then continued up the track towards the western slope and the far end of Bophelong. It was the direction of the Dikobe house.
10 As it went out of sight over the top of the rise, Naledi felt sick.

A man from the van raised a large *megaphone* to his mouth:

megaphone

"No one is to leave the village. We are here to find
15 the *terrorist* who burned the chief's house. You must all stay in your homes until we say you can go. Anyone trying to leave will be shot!"

Policemen went off in different directions, their *rifles* forward, while the white officer spoke into a radio
20 that he held close to his face.

The *queue* of people at the tap remained still.

---

van, a car with no side windows used for transporting goods or people
terrorist, a person who takes part in *terrorism*, that is the use of violence for political reasons
rifle ['raɪfl], see picture, page 45
queue [kjuː], line (of people)

44

rifle

"You heard! Hurry up! Go home!" a policeman shouted.

Everybody needed the day's water. Could they not get their water first? They looked uncertainly at the policeman. A couple of small frightened children ran away from the line crying, their empty buckets swinging and knocking their legs. With a small nod, the policeman told the rest that they could take one bucket of water each.

The other policemen were going out between the houses, shouting the order to stay indoors. The man with the megaphone continued to shout his message out further up the village.

On the way home Naledi and Tiro caught sight of a great truck approaching the village but still some distance away. It slowed down and a couple of figures jumped off. Then it continued across the veld, stopping every now and again to let more figures out. They seemed to be making a ring around the village.

When they had their water Naledi and Tiro went home. From the window next to Nono's bed they could see up to the church. But the place Naledi was thinking about most was out of sight - Taolo's house. The police van had been going that way. In the distance they occasionally caught sight of figures carrying guns. Their clothes seemed to be almost the same colour as

45

the veld. The police within the village were moving from house to house, starting furthest from the centre and coming inward. That meant they would come to Nono's house towards the end.

5   The hours passed. It was terrible not knowing what was happening. Then Tiro called Naledi into the side room.

"They're over there!" he whispered.

He pointed to the Sadires' house. A policeman was
10 going towards it with his rifle. It would be their turn soon. At the same moment a loud shout was followed by David Sadire, the older boy, *stumbling* out of the door at the front. A policeman appeared close behind, his rifle at David's back forcing him in the direction of
15 the church. What could David have done? He was so quiet and hardworking, certainly not outspoken like Taolo.

Chapter 11

"What do you know about the fire at the chief's house?"

20 "Are you friendly with the Dikobe people?"

"What did you discuss with Mma Tshadi?"

"Are you the one who's making trouble in school?"

"Why don't you answer?"

The man firing the questions at Naledi in a low, sure
25 voice did not seem to be just an ordinary policeman, the sort who simply beat and pushed people around. He was not carrying a rifle like the other man who was

stumble, to fall or almost fall

searching the house. Instead, he had a small gun in a leather bag at his *waist*. He knew a lot about the village, and he stared at Naledi as he asked each question. He would wait for a few seconds for an answer and then break the silence with another question. 5

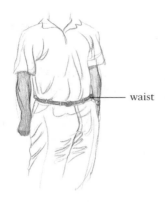

waist

"Why don't you answer? If you don't talk to me, I shall have to take you to my boss."

It was Nono who saved her.

"Why do you ask my granddaughter so many questions? Can't you see that I am sick? The child hasn't 10 time for anything but her studies and looking after us all here. Young man, why don't you go and ask your questions of people who have time to run around in the streets?"

Nono's voice was not angry, simply calm and reason- 15 able. Where did she get this sudden strength from?

The man looked at her. "These aren't children's games I'm talking about now. These children today are

---

search, to look carefully in order to find something

47

getting mixed up in big matters they don't understand. It's dangerous. If we don't teach them to leave these things alone, they'll get hurt and many families will be crying."

5 "I know what you are speaking about, young man, and you are right that many families are crying. But I'm saying to you that this child of mine here doesn't have time for these things."

"You are lucky to have such a good grandmother," 10 the policeman said in a sharp tone. "You'd be *stupid* to get mixed up with this politics business, because you will only hurt yourself and your family. Terrorists get help in villages like this one. They start with setting fire to a chief's house, next thing it's a police station. 15 But we have already found some troublemakers here and they will soon be happy to tell us what they know. You see, we find out everyting in the end, so I'm giving you a warning. If I have questions to ask you another time, I will make sure you answer them."

20 He nodded to the man with the rifle to follow him outside. Then he turned back towards the door. "Good-bye, Mma," he said, and without waiting for Nono to reply he walked off.

As soon as he had gone, Naledi took her 25 grandmother's hand. "If you hadn't spoken, Nono, he would have taken me! They surely have Taolo! What do they want with David Sadire? They are just trying to frighten us!"

"My child," Nono said, "the policeman was right 30 that these things are dangerous and bring many tears. It's better to leave them alone. I hope God will change

stupid, slow to learn and understand things

48

the hearts of those who are so hard to poor people like us."

"Nono, what they are doing to us... it's wrong, it's bad! How can we sit and do nothing?"

Nono did not reply. 5

"I won't do anything silly, Nono, don't worry!" Naledi said.

Tiro, who had been standing by the entrance to the small side room all the time, now broke the silence. "I hate them!" he said. 10

****

The moment the police van began driving out of the village, doors opened wide and details of the *raid* passed quickly over the yards. The ring of soldiers around the village had been ordered back into the truck.

Naledi and Tiro hurried out with buckets for the 15 tap. Stopping first at the Sadire house, they found David's four younger brothers and sisters inside. Their mother had left early in the morning for work in the town, before the police had arrived. The eldest girl, about Tiro's age, said the policeman with the small gun 20 had shouted at David that they would find out every-thing about the fire. David had said that he knew nothing about it until that morning. The policeman had hit him on the mouth and said that he was lying. Then they had taken David away. 25

Naledi told the children to wait in their

---

raid, a surprise visit by the police, etc, to arrest people

grandfather's house. Their mother would return later in the evening.

The news was discussed at the water tap. People said Mma Tshadi had been taken away. Others had seen both Saul Dikobe and his son being forced into the van. Naledi left the bucket with Tiro and ran off to the Dikobe house. There she found Mma Dikobe packing a small bag.

"I wanted to come and see your grandmother before leaving for Jo'burg. You've heard about Saul and Taolo? I want to talk to Saul's *lawyer* immediately and see what can be done. I'm glad they didn't take you too. They just take anyone and beat them up until they get the answers they want."

Walking back through the village with Mma Dikobe, Naledi felt that she didn't care what the policeman had said. She was glad to be walking beside her.

When they reached the house, Mma Dikobe sat down next to Nono, talking calmly as if her only worry was how the old lady was feeling and getting on. At last Mma Dikobe said that she was glad the medicine was taking effect and that with plenty of rest Nono would soon get well. As she was counting out more tablets onto the table, Mma Kau arrived.

"Did the police also trouble you, Mma? Is your son alright?" Naledi asked.

"He... he wasn't there when the police came. Last night he told me he had to go back to work right away."

"But Mma, he only just came home."

---

lawyer ['lɔɪə], a person trained in the law who does legal work for other people

50

"Can you make some tea, Naledi?" Mma Dikobe asked. "I'm sure the police have already asked Mma Kau enough questions."

While they drank the tea, Mma Kau hardly spoke. Nor did she really seem to notice Dineo when she came to greet her. Yesterday she had been so strong and sure, helping out their family. Today Mma Kau herself was in need of help. Something must have happened to her son. Why had he left so suddenly? Naledi remembered his silent face as he stood at the back of the crowd outside the chief's house the previous afternoon, and in that moment she knew what must be in Mma Kau's mind. Looking at Mma Dikobe and Nono, Naledi felt they knew too.

Mma Dikobe left late in the afternoon. She said she was not sure when she would return.

Chapter 12

Dear Mma,

Sitting at the table in the lamplight, Naledi tried to finish a letter to her mother, far away in Jo'burg:

I don't know what will happen about the move,
Mma. Most people say we should refuse to go.
But we don't even know when they will send
the trucks. I know it's hard for you to leave
your work, so I will just have to write to let
you know what is happening. We all think
about you.

There was so much more Naledi wanted to tell her mother, so much she had left out. She had not mentioned school, nor her contact with the Dikobes. It was not just that she did not want to add to Mma's worries. From her friend Grace she had learned to be careful about putting things on paper. Letters could be opened by the police. They could be sent on after they had been read and copied, and you might not even know.

The following day Mma Tshadi returned on foot and alone. She and the Dikobes and David Sadire had been kept overnight in the local police *cells* in Boomdal. Early in the morning, a white man, not in police uniform, had ordered her release. No explanation had been given and she had no further news about the others.

In the days that followed, Naledi's mind was often far away, imagining what might be happening to Taolo, his father and David Sadire in some police station somewhere.

Returning to school the day after the raid, Naledi prepared to say a meaningless 'I'm sorry' to Mr Molaba. The raid had helped make up her mind. There seemed no point in not doing so. She would only get expelled and it would not change anything. It would only stop her from meeting other students. School was the only place where they had any chance of getting together to discuss things. But Mr Molaba did not even call her to his office. Had he forgotten? Or was he leaving her alone for a purpose? What if he had asked one of the students to spy on her? She would have to be careful.

Something, however, had changed at school. On the surface the students still seemed to be working

---

cell, a very small room in a prison

52

hard under Molaba's rule, but remarks were being made, looks were being exchanged. Everyone seemed to know about the raid on Bophelong and the arrests. Taolo's name was mentioned in whispers.

At breaktime Mr Molaba *patrolled* the school yard, making it impossible for any group of students to get together for serious discussions. Miriam joined Naledi beside the wire fence. Naledi was talking in a low voice when quite unexpectedly, two of the older students who had been present at Naledi's beating came up to them, one of them calling out, "Why do you look out in the road when you've got *handsome* fellows like us inside here?!"

"Come on! At least you can talk to us!" said the other.

"Maybe they won't because we never told them our names!" laughed the first.

"No problem! He's Zach and I'm Dan!"

The first boy whispered quickly, "Laugh as if we've made a joke. Molaba is watching us."

In between loud talk and laughing the boys gave them their message: Some of the top class students were planning to get the head's *permission* to hold a students' *prayer* meeting, and they would then arrange for Mr Molaba to be called away at the same time. If they put a *nail* into one of his car *tyres*, he would want

---

patrol, to go round an area to check that it is safe and that there is no trouble or danger
handsome ['hænsəm], (of a man) good looking
permission, the action of allowing somebody to do something
prayer, words to express a wish or thanks to God
nail, *tyre*, see picture, page 54

nail　　　tyre

to change it at once, as he always liked to leave school on time. Then the students could discuss plans to *resist* the removal.

"Tell all your friends to attend the prayer meeting," Dan whispered.

To Naledi's surprise Mr Molaba agreed at once to the prayer meeting. She had thought he might see through the idea, but it appeared that he was pleased that some of his students were showing an interest in religion. Nor did he *suspect* anything when they asked if *Rev.* Radebe could lead the meeting. Rev. Radebe was well known as a popular *priest* in the community. When Rev. Radebe was *elected* as one of the people's *representatives* on the Boomdal *Resistance* Committee that weekend, it would be too late for Mr Molaba to change his mind without looking *foolish*. After all, the students

resist, to offer opposition; to refuse to agree
suspect, to have an idea that something is wrong or not true without being able to prove it
Rev. (Reverend) ['revərənd],the title of a *priest or minister*, that is a person performing religious duties in a Christian church.
elect, to chose somebody by voting
representative, one who represents another or others
resistance, the action of using force to show one is against something or somebody
foolish, silly

54

had only asked for the priest to lead them in prayers.

As the day of the meeting drew near, it became clear that so many students wanted to attend that a class-room would be too small. Mr Molaba agreed that it could be held in the front yard. Fortunately his car was always parked at the back of the school, so if he could only be kept busy there, he would be out of the way.

On the day, Rev. Radebe arrived as the bell rang for break. Crowds of students came down the steps from their classrooms. Naledi put her pen into a pocket. A message had been passed around that everyone should bring a pen or pencil as well as their *hymn* books.

Mr Molaba and the priest greeted each other and together they walked up the steps to where Mr Mola-ba usually stood high above them at *assembly*.

"I am pleased to welcome Rev. Radebe here today," Mr Molaba said, "and I am happy to see that so many children in my school wish to spend this breaktime in prayer. As you know I have been worried that some of you might be led into foolishness and so destroy your-selves. I am glad to see that you have not forgotten God. That said, I will now hand you over to Rev. Radebe."

"Thank you, headmaster. I too was very glad when your students came to me with this idea of a prayer meeting. These are difficult times and God is there to give us strength if only we call on him. So let us begin today by singing one of my favourite hymns, 'Onward Christian Soldiers.'"

hymn [hɪm], a religious song
assembly, a gathering of the students and teachers in a school at the start or end of the day

Hymn books were opened and pages turned, when two students came hurrying from behind the classroom block. One of the boys went up to Mr Molaba and spoke in a low but clear whisper.

5 "Excuse us, sir. We were coming from the toilets and we noticed your car has a flat tyre at the front."

The headmaster turned to Rev. Radebe. "Will you excuse me? I had better go and look at this right away."

He signalled to the two students who had brought 10 the news. "Come with me."

The students started singing: "Onward, Christian Soldiers, marching as to war."

Rev. Radebe talked about *courage*. About Moses and the Jews keeping their *faith* while *slaves* in Egypt; about 15 the early Christians in the powerful Roman state; about all those who had suffered death.

"It is in your hearts that God plants his message. You must listen very carefully to it."

Naledi felt as if her mind were in flames. He was 20 talking about their own situation. He told them to have the courage to do what they themselves believed was right.

"What I'm saying to you is not easy. There are also other important qualities that we need besides courage. 25 This is where your pens come in. I've asked some of my young friends to give out some paper, and I want each of you to write down the five qualities you think are

---

courage ['kʌrɪdʒ], the ability to control fear when facing danger, pain, opposition, etc
faith, strong religious belief; trust
slave, a person who is legally owned by somebody and is forced to work for them

most important for any human being. I like to know what young people are thinking. Please don't discuss the matter with your neighbour. Just think about it yourself very quietly. You will have three minutes and then you hand your papers in." 5

Pieces of paper passed rapidly along the lines. Naledi looked at the paper. Printed down the side were the numbers one to five, and at the top were these words:

THIS IS YOUR CHANCE TO ELECT THE
STUDENTS YOU WANT TO REPRESENT YOU 10
IN OUR STRUGGLE AGAINST REMOVAL.
WRITE THE NAMES OF FIVE STUDENTS.

So this was what it was all about! A meeting to elect representatives! Did Rev. Radebe know this, or had the organizers replaced the papers without his knowl- 15
edge? Whoever had done it certainly had courage.

Naledi wrote down five names, starting with Taolo Dikobe. Just because he was expelled and the police had got him at the moment should not stop him being a representative. She hoped others would think the 20
same way. As the papers were being gathered, Mr Molaba came back. Rev. Radebe was quick to explain what he had asked to students to do. Then he said a final prayer.

Chapter 13

From the moment Zach called Naledi aside in the school yard the following day to say she had been elected onto the student committee, something changed in her. There was no longer time simply to sit and wonder what was happening to Taolo in prison, or what was going to happen to them all. News of who had been elected spread rapidly through the school, and before she had time even to think about what it would mean to be a student representative, people were coming to her with their *complaints* and *suggestions*. If Mr Molaba was observing the yard, he would surely see something was up, but there was no time even to worry about that.

Naledi's election took her by surprise. It must be, she supposed, because of the beating and the connection with Taolo. There had been a big vote for him even though he had been expelled and was held by the police. Zach and Dan had both been elected, as well as a girl called Theresa from the top class. There were at least five more popular names, so that if anyone were arrested, someone else could step in. A boy in Naledi's class, Ben Mosai, would work in Taolo's place until he was released from prison. The first meeting of the student committee was arranged for the next day straight after school at Zach's house. His mother and the neighbours would be out at work. Since any meeting needed permission from the authorities, they would have to be careful.

They all sat down at the kitchen table in the main

complaint, a reason for not being satisfied
suggestion, an idea or plan that is being suggested

58

room. There was only one other room with hardly any space between the table and a bed along the wall. A curtain had been pulled across the room to divide it. Zach saw Naledi looking at the curtain and explained, "My older sister and her husband live with us, but they don't come back until late." 5

Then, giving his younger brother and sister a couple of cents each, Zach told them to play outside and keep watch for him.

Zach was businesslike. "It's not safe to be here more than half an hour, so we must work quickly. This is our 10 first student committee meeting and we want everyone in Boomdal to see what we can do when we act together. We could start with a march from school to the Boomdal Council offices and from there to the white people's Town Hall. Dan and I have been speaking to 15 students, and nearly all of them want to show openly that they are against this removal. It's time we stopped being pushed around."

Dan explained that the route of the march would go past the primary school so those children could also 20 join in. It would be peaceful, with students only carrying *placards*.

"Everybody must see what we think about this removal. Our parents and the old people must know that we're determined not to move. There's no other 25 way."

It was decided that immediately after assembly on the following Monday, instead of marching into class, the students would all turn around and march out of 30

| *placard* ['plækɑ:d], see picture, page 66

59

the school. Zach's elder brother had a van that could be parked outside the gates and in which the placards could be hidden.

Each of the five agreed on what was to be done before Monday. Naledi's main task was to inform students from the first class in their school and to make contact with the primary school. They would aim to walk past during the morning break. Tiro and Zach's brother and sister could tell a few children whom they trusted to tell others to join the marchers. Within half an hour the meeting was over.

Walking quickly along the track back to Bophelong, Naledi was not sure whether she felt more excited or nervous. To her Soweto friend Grace and to Taolo, protest marches were nothing new. But however much she had heard about them, actually helping to organize and take part in one herself was like stepping into the unknown.

Naledi had told Nono that she would be a little late because she had to help Mr Gwala to clear up. She hated lying to her grandmother, but it would be impossible to tell the truth without causing her yet more worry. Hadn't she promised Nono she would not do anything stupid? What she was doing now wasn't at all stupid.

Later Naledi spoke quietly to Tiro about the plans for the march, explaining how they were to be kept *secret* in case teachers and parents tried to stop it. Tiro was certain that younger children as well as those from his class and the other higher classes would want to join.

| *secret*, (a thing) that must not be known by other people

60

"Do you think they'll shoot?" Tiro asked.

Naledi did not reply. It was something she had not wanted to think about. She knew it had happened in other places, but if they began to let those thoughts frighten them, they would never make any protest at all but just give in to everything. They were only planning to carry posters. Was it right, though, to let the younger primary children come? When the government sent its trucks to move them, everyone would be thrown onto them, little children too. They were all caught up in something much bigger than themselves. No one was safe. Why couldn't all the adults see this? Nono would say you might as well give in, for the sake of peace. But where was peace?

Chapter 14

On Sunday Nono said she was well enough to go to church.

"We must pray to God to help us now," she said. "Yes, we shall pray, Mma Modibe," Mma Tshadi said, "but praying by itself is not enough. We shall need others to come to help us."

Rra Rampou told Nono, "They can kill me first. They won't take me alive from here." Many villagers, as well as workers living on white-owned farms in the district, regularly attended the church on Sundays. It was a chance to share worries and exchange news.

Supporting her grandmother up the steps of the old stone church's doorway she saw a familiar figure halfway down the path, walking in their direction.

"Mma Dikobe's back, Nono!"

61

Nono turned, smiling, before she continued into the church.

Mma Dikobe found a seat behind them. They just had time to exchange greetings before the priest arrived. When the service was over, Mma Dikobe came to take Nono's arm.

"How is it with you, Mma? Shouldn't you still be resting?"

As they came out of the building into the bright sunshine of the yard, other villagers greeted Mma Dikobe. People who had previously been afraid to talk to the Dikobe family now showed pleasure at her return.

"What news do you bring of your husband and your son, Mma?" Mma Tshadi asked.

Mma Dikobe looked down as she answered, perhaps hiding the pain in her eyes. "The only news I have is that they are in Modderbee Prison. It took a whole week just to find that out. Saul's lawyer tried to get permission to see him, but they won't let him in."

She too had been to the prison and to the police *headquarters* in Johannesburg. All she had been told was that there were no charges yet against the two of them, but they were being held under the Terrorism Act and could be kept for as long as the police wanted.

When Mma Dikobe finished speaking, Mma Tshadi took her hand. "You are part of our family now, Mma. It was very wrong of us to treat you like unwelcome strangers. Yesterday I sent two of my children to give your plants water. They were growing so nicely before you left. The children will come and help you carry

---

headquarters, a place from which an organization is controlled, especially the police and army; the head office

water and also do weeding if you wish. It's not easy to be on your own."

The other women also wanted to help. For the first time Naledi saw tears in Mma Dikobe's eyes.

"I was without my husband for a long time. It's hard- er now because my son is gone as well. If your children come, I'll be glad to see them. Thank you, Mma." Excusing herself from the small gathering, Mma Dikobe took Nono's arm. "Let me take you home, Mma."

****

Naledi found it hard to fall asleep that night. She lay thinking about the march, trying to imagine what might happen. The sound of rain on the roof helped her to sleep at last.

Usually Tiro set off well before Naledi, but on this Monday morning, after getting the water, Naledi prepared to leave with him. Nono noticed but said nothing, watching Naledi from her bed. Mma Dikobe had told her not to return to work for at least another week, promising to write a letter to the farmer. With luck the job would be kept for her.

If Nono asked why she was leaving so early, Naledi had again planned to say that Mr Gwala needed some help in the school garden. Nono said nothing, but as they said goodbye, there was a look in her grandmother's eyes that was not angry but very, very sad.

Chapter 15

Naledi and Tiro joined a group of children on their way to school.

"Has your headmaster sent you back to primary school?" one of the children asked Naledi.

5 "Don't be stupid! She's a student representative now!" said Tiro. "There's a big march today. They'll all come right past our school so we can join it."

Naledi explained why they weren't told earlier, making it clear that the teachers should not be told in 10 case they then forced them to stay indoors.

The five high school representatives met behind the general store. Naledi was the first to arrive. She was very nervous. If something happened to her and Tiro, how would Nono manage? What if the others also had 15 second thoughts about the march and were backing out? Then she saw Zach and Dan coming. She was no longer alone. With the arrival of Theresa and Ben shortly afterwards, they were complete - and ready for action.

20 Zach's brother would park his van with the posters outside the school just before assembly time. Both Zach and Dan would stand at the back of their class lines, nearest the gates, to lead the students out and hand them placards as they passed. The signal would 25 be when Mr Molaba began his usual "Good morning, children." That would be the moment for them to shout, "We march," and begin to walk out.

In the school yard the students were very excited. Surely Mr Molaba would suspect something. Suddenly 30 he called to Mr Gwala and pulled his keys from his pocket. He pushed them into the teacher's hand while

64

whispering something to him. Mr Gwala began walking somewhat slowly towards the gates. Was he going to lock them? There was no time to lose. Naledi was not sure who shouted first, but within seconds the cry "We march" sounded and the students moved quickly 5 towards the gates.

"Run, Gwala!" the headmaster shouted. But he was not running. Instead he was standing well back from the crowd shouting something himself like "Slow down!". There was a danger people would get crushed 10 going through the gates all at once. Naledi found herself being pushed through the gate. Zach and Dan were already further down the road running towards an old green van with its back doors open. As the students went by, placards were handed out rapidly and were 15 lifted up high.

NO REMOVALS!
WE WON'T GO!
RELEASE TAOLO DIKOBE!
WE SAY NO TO BOP! 20
LEAVE US IN PEACE!
APARTHEID MUST GO - NOT US!

People looked up as they watched the students pass. Dogs and small children ran excitedly beside them; the owner of the general store came outside with his cus- 25 tomers; a group of jobless young men stopped their game of cards to stare and shout comments. Everyone was taking notice!

Songs begun by students at the front spread along the entire length of the thick line of a few hundred stu- 30 dents. All of Boomdal could surely hear them.

Turning the corner, Naledi saw primary children already running down the road to join them. Seconds

placard

later, it was all over. At its far end the road was filled
by figures in uniform with dogs in front of them.

A warning message was passed back through the
crowd as more children came over the locked gate and
5 fence of the primary school, not realizing the danger
from the other direction. Naledi could not see Tiro but
felt certain he was marching with the others. They
were all shouting "We won't move."

They were close enough to see that apart from the men with dogs, many of the black police were carrying *whips*, the terrible **sjamboks**. There were a few white policemen among yet more black policemen in between vans parked on the open veld to the left. Here 5 they had rifles. What should they do? The Council offices were off a road further down to the right. They were slowing down until Zach's voice was heard calling for a *halt*. Only a couple of hundred metres now lay between them and the police. 10

whip

Someone shouted, "This is a peaceful march! Let us through!"

The cry was taken up by voices all around. Could a couple of representatives not talk to the police, explain it was only a peaceful *demonstration*? A shout came 15 from the policemen and suddenly barking dogs came

halt, a short stop
demonstration, a public meeting or march protesting against or supporting somebody or something

running towards them. As the dogs were pulling down the first victims, policemen with raised sjamboks ran into the mass of screaming students. The only way out was onto the veld, where the police lines were thinner.

Suddenly a dog jumped at Naledi and caught her dress. She pulled it away but the thin material was *ripped*. She felt a sjambok across her shoulder and arms. She fell and rolled over in pain, hands over her head. She was going to be crushed... until she felt hands lifting her and pulling her away. It was student committee member Ben Mosai helping her to get away.

Students were *bleeding*, lying injured on the ground; others were still fighting with the police and their dogs; some were being pulled into vans while others were running and throwing stones. There were sounds of shots in the air.

"It's okay... I'm all right," Naledi told Ben.

"It's not safe here. Come further!"

The main police attack was moving further down the road close to the primary school, where children were now climbing the fence, trying to get back inside. Others were running into yards and houses to hide.

But not for long. A large number of black policemen led by a white officer approached the school gates. A teacher in the yard who was telling the children to hurry inside was called to the gates. She talked to the police. Then she returned to the building. A minute later the head teacher appeared. It was clear that he didn't want to let the police into his school. In the end

rip, to pull apart or into pieces
bleed, to lose blood

68

he took the keys from his pocket and slowly opened the gates.

It was important to find houses where people could take the injured students before the police began to put them into their trucks. And how could the injured be taken to hospital? Their student committee had not planned for such things. There was no time to lose. News about Tiro would have to wait.

Soon students who could not walk were being carried indoors. Some had deep long cuts from sjamboks, others had been badly *bitten* by the dogs. She was shocked to find Theresa with an open head wound. Her own pain did not seem so bad anymore. How could people with eyes, ears and hearts do such things to other human beings?

As the last of the injured were being brought in, Dan and some of the others set off to find transport to the hospital. It was possible that the police would go there to look for them, but many of the wounds needed to be taken care of immediately. They would have to take the risk.

When Naledi came home, Dineo was sitting in the yard with her *doll*. She stared at her sister's dress.

"Tiro? Is he here?" Naledi asked.

"No." Then Naledi saw her grandmother's thin figure appear at the door. Things were not working out and she could not even tell Nono where Tiro was. All she could say was, "We had to do it, Nono! We had to!"

---

bite, to cut into something with the *teeth*, see picture, page
doll, a model of a human figure, especially a baby or a child, for a child to play with

Chapter 16

Nono remained silent. Naledi sat down. She tried to explain to Nono what had happened, how the march was meant to be peaceful, how the police had started attacking them, how she had seen Tiro running away.

5   When Naledi had repaired her dress she asked her grandmother to let her go back to Boomdal to look again for Tiro.

"He might need my help now." But Nono shook her head. The look in Nono's eyes cut like a knife.

10 "Why did you not think of helping your brother before? What good is it now? Did you imagine the police would stand looking at all of you? You think that someone as old as I am knows nothing?"

The effort of speaking had been too much for Nono.
15 As she tried to get up from her chair her legs failed her. Naledi ran forward to support her and led her step by step to the bed. Nothing more was said. Nono's angry words were worse than either the policemen's sjambok or Mr Molaba's cane. Those just hurt her body, but
20 these hurt her heart.

The silence in the house was broken in the early evening when Mma Kau called on her way back from visiting her sister in Boomdal. Her sister lived well beyond the Council offices, so they had not seen any-
25 thing, but news of the police attack on the students had spread like wildfire. Children from a number of families were either injured or missing, and people in Boomdal were angry with the police. She told them how people had been helping many children by letting
30 them hide inside their houses. Tiro could still be in hiding. But if he had not returned by the following

70

morning, she promised to go herself to the hospital and
to Boomdal police station.

Nono seemed to become a little calmer as she listened to Mma Kau, and her mention of the hospital
gave Naledi an idea.

"Mma Dikobe may have seen Tiro if he went to the
hospital! Let me go and ask her, please, Nono! She
should be home by now," Naledi said.

"Let her go, Mma," put in Mma Kau. "She won't be
away for long."

But Mma Dikobe's house was dark and empty. She
was usually home by this time. Had she stayed behind
in the hospital to help with all the injured students?
Naledi felt that she too should be in Boomdal helping
those who had been hurt.

Mma Kau had gone when Naledi returned. "It's still
dark in her house," she said quietly.

Dineo was asleep beside Nono on the bed. Naledi
had something to eat and then prepared to sleep. It was
the first time she could remember the mat beside her
being empty. She felt alone even though Nono and
Dineo were only on the other side of the doorway.
What hurt her so much was that look in Nono's eyes -
as if she were the cause of Tiro's being in trouble. Nono
just did not understand. And what would their mother
think? She might say that Naledi as an older sister
should have tried to stop Tiro from becoming involved
in the march. But if they all started worrying about pro-
tecting only themselves and their own family, they
would never be able to change anything. How could
they ever fight against an *enemy* that had so much pow-

---

enemy ['enəmɪ], a person who wants to injure or attack somebody

71

er over them unless they all joined together? They had so much to learn and a lot of them were going to be hurt.

She would have to be hard if she was going to get through this thing. Tiro had been changing. If the police caught him now, she could not imagine him giving in to them. They would probably kill him first with their *tortures*. Terrible images came to her mind of Tiro's broken body on a cold prison floor.

Naledi woke as she heard a soft knocking. Already Nono was getting out of bed next door.

"Wait, Nono, I'll go," she called. It was dark and she felt her way to the door. There, with Mma Dikobe's arm around his shoulders, was Tiro!

"We're lucky to have this one back," said Mma Dikobe. Nono took Tiro in her arms.

"What's wrong with your leg?" Nono asked. Before he could reply, Mma Dikobe took Nono's arm and sat her down.

"Don't worry, Mma. He's all right," Mma Dikobe's face was tired.

Mma Dikobe told the story. The hospital was full of injured students and she was called from her normal duties to help. In the middle of the afternoon police came in demanding to see who was being treated. They took away a number of the older students for questioning, including one girl with a serious head wound. When a nurse tried to stop them from pulling the girl from a bed, she was told to mind her own business or she too would be arrested. Not even the white doctor

torture, the action or practice of causing somebody serious pain in order to force them to say or do something

72

could stop them. It appeared the police were also looking for a younger child, a boy with a foot wound from a
dog bite. The hospital was told to report any such case
being brought to them.

But Mma Dikobe had seen Tiro in the waiting area 5
and immediately took him over. She took care of his
wound herself. No record card was filled in and Tiro's
teacher agreed to take him back to her house until
Mma Dikobe could come for him later. The night-time
journey on foot back to Bophelong had been very slow. 10
They could have taken a taxi, but Mma Dikobe
thought it safer to walk and not be seen by anybody.

When Mma Dikobe finished speaking, Nono raised
her tired eyes.

"I thank God for that teacher and for you, Mma. But 15
what about all those children now in prison? Who can
help their parents get them back? It's too hard for
someone old like me to understand. Won't you sleep
here with us, Mma? It's late to go to your house."

Mma Dikobe thanked Nono but said she must 20
return home. Before leaving she told Tiro to stay in the
house until he could walk better so no one would
notice his wound.

Settling down for the second time that night, Naledi lay close to Tiro so they could whisper very quietly 25
without Nono hearing, but they were too tired to talk
for long and they soon fell asleep.

Chapter 17

As Naledi was getting ready for school, Nono spoke to her. "Must you go today? Why don't you stay with your brother?"

"I must go, but I'll be careful," Naledi said.

5 Nono turned away, appearing not to hear when Naledi said good-bye.

On her way she passed what was left of the Sekete house. Already the fire seemed to have happened a long time ago though it was only two weeks. With no
10 other students in sight, Naledi walked quickly, leaving the fields and entering the veld. She sensed something was wrong as she approached the store. Students were walking away from the school.

"No school! We have to go home!" someone called
15 to her.

The school gates were shut and various students were gathered outside. There was a notice on the inside of the fence:

NO *UNAUTHORIZED* PERSON
20 IS ALLOWED
ON THE SCHOOL GROUNDS
OR
IN THE SCHOOL BUILDINGS

The whole school closed! One march by the stu-
25 dents, which they were not even allowed to complete, and their school was shut down! For how long? Was this part of the removal plan? The students outside the

---

unauthorized, for which official permission is not given

74

gates asked each other these questions.

"I live near Mr Gwala," Miriam said. "The police were at his house last night for more than an hour. But they didn't take him."

Perhaps the police were looking for an adult who 5 could have helped the students organize their protest. Naledi thought of Rev. Radebe. Had the police made that connection yet?

"They're looking for all the organizers. You should be careful," said a student from the top class to Naledi. 10 She was the only one of the five representatives there. Theresa was probably the girl the police had taken from the hospital. But where were Zach, Dan and Ben? No one knew.

If Naledi went to the primary school, she might be 15 able to speak to Zach's brother or sister during the first break. She would have to hurry if she were to reach the primary children before they went back into class. Hearing running footsteps behind her, she turned to find Miriam. 20

"Where are you going? Can I help?"

They were in time. Playtime shouts and cries carried down the same road they had marched along yesterday. Arriving at the fence, Naledi called to a couple of children and a few seconds later her message had been 25 taken and Zach's sister came running over. They hadn't seen Zach since the previous morning, before the march, although a note had been put under the door during the night. It said he was okay and would come home when it was safe. Her mother had sent her 30 to Dan's house and Dan's family had received a similar note. The police had been in their house in the evening. One of the police had shouted at their mother to

tell him what she knew or he would take them all to prison. Perhaps he had realized from their expressions that they really did not know, because after turning the house upside down, they left as suddenly as they had
5 come.

"What will you do?" Miriam asked as they left the school yard. "They'll come for you."

Naledi was afraid that her grandmother might have another attack if she *disappeared* into hiding. But that
10 could also happen if she didn't hide and was arrested. It was not only a question of Nono and the family. What were the students going to do about continuing their resistance? They could not let it be crushed just because the school had been closed. It was important
15 to organize something outside school. They needed an organization of young people to work with the Boom-dal Resistance Committee. Bophelong also needed to prepare itself. The removal could not be stopped by talking. There was so much to do...

20 "You can stay at my house," Miriam said. "We can tell my parents that your grandmother is in hospital and you have nowhere to stay. If we tell them the police are looking for you, they might be afraid to hide you."

25 Fear ... it was everywhere. You had to push against it as Miriam was doing.

"Thanks, but I must go home. I can't leave Nono just like that. Maybe the police don't know everything. If they wanted me, why didn't they come last night
30 when they were looking for Zach and Dan? Or they could have picked me up outside school this morning.

---

disappear, to be lost, or impossible to find or see

76

Miriam wasn't sure, but Naledi had made up her mind. There were times for running away but this was not one of them.

Chapter 18

Arriving at the road on the other side of the veld, Naledi stopped. Why go home immediately? It was still 5 morning. If she turned right instead of left, the road led to the hospital. She could find out how many students were there. She also needed very much to talk to Mma Dikobe. There would probably be little chance of talking to her by herself. All the nurses would be terribly 10 busy.

A long queue of people were standing and sitting alongside the wall of one of the buildings.

A white woman in an office looked at Naledi with her blue eyes. 15

"Yes?" the woman said in English.

"I ... I've come to see Mma ... I mean Nurse Dikobe." Naledi was looking for the words in English.

"What is it that you want? She's working at the moment." 20

"It ... it's personal."

"Well, I can't promise. They're very busy in there and she's already had to leave her work once this morning to take a telephone call. Wait here and I'll see. What's your name?" 25

Naledi told her.

The white woman returned.

"You'll have to wait. She'll come when she's free."

Naledi thanked her. She had not been told to wait outside so she sat down quietly.

At last Mma Dikobe arrived.

"What's wrong, Naledi?"

5 "They shut our school, Mma. I thought I could talk to you here, and maybe help."

A smile passed across Mma Dikobe's face as she thanked Naledi, but added that it would be difficult.

"So the school has been closed? That's a bad sign."

10 "Can I come to your house tonight to speak to you, Mma?"

Mma Dikobe nodded. "Yes, come. I may even have a big surprise for you. This morning there was a phone call from Saul's lawyer. He's heard that Taolo and Saul 15 have been released. They may be coming home tonight."

"Oh, Mma! That's wonderful news! I'll be seeing you all tonight!"

Chapter 19

Telling Nono about the closing of the school was not 20 easy. Nono, who had never been to school herself, had managed to keep their father in school for only three years when he was young. There had been no money for more. Nono had said that school was like a river, offering its water only to those lucky few who could 25 stay beside it. Naledi's mother wanted to do all she could to keep her children beside the river, and in turn, they would have to work very hard to drink as much from it as possible.

78

How could Nono understand the students' feelings? Although she was so worried by the idea of removal, she still could not accept that young people should risk schooling by trying to resist.

When Naledi had once repeated her grandmother's story to Taolo, he had said, "But why must we learn *Afrikaans* and just those things the government want us to know? A government we can't even vote for! So they can keep us where they want forever! No! We must get to the source of the river, clean it up and make new courses for it. Then we'll send it all over the dry land!"

Naledi sat down to eat a little, then she said she was going out to collect more firewood at the riverbed. When no one else was there, that was one place where Naledi always felt at peace. She remembered the time when it had been full of water. That was before the white farmer had started to use the water on his farm. Villagers still spoke of their shock at losing their water supply. Until the pipeline had been laid to the village, they had to make the long journey with buckets to the white farm to buy water that they had once taken freely from the river.

On her way back, Naledi thought of the Dikobe family. Had Taolo and his father returned?

Mma Dikobe had already arrived, as promised, to check Tiro's foot. "Forgive me, Mma," she said to Nono when Naledi arrived, "I have something on my mind. I must hurry now. If Naledi comes with me, she can collect some more *bandages* from my house. Then

---

Afrikaans, a language developed from Ducth, spoken by whites is S. A.
bandage ['bændɪdʒ], see picture, page 80

79

bandage

she can change it for her brother tomorrow."

They reached the Dikobe house before it was completely dark. Inside, Mma Dikobe lit the lamp. The house was large compared with Nono's, with three rooms leading off the main one. Then Naledi thought she heard the sound of a motor. They both went to the door. Yes, they could see the headlights of a car in the distance! Quickly Mma Dikobe pulled Naledi back.

"It's better the police don't see you here!"

Naledi hurried outside to the back of the house. She could hear the car stopping and people getting out of it. A loud voice announced in English, "You didn't think you'd see this place so soon, did you, hey? We're being good to you. But any trouble and you'll be back in prison before you can say your own name!"

There was no reply. Naledi heard only the silence of the night and her own heart beating very fast.

"Well, hello, Mma Dikobe! Aren't you going to greet your husband and son?"

"I can wait until you leave."

Whatever she was feeling, Mma Dikobe's voice was calm.

"It seems we're not welcome here, gentlemen! I thought the lady should thank us for returning her family! One last word. Your husband is under twenty-four-hour house arrest, so he must stay inside this fence.

And remember, our eyes and ears are everywhere. Every move you make, even in a little place like this, we'll know about it!"

"Let's go!"

Naledi stayed where she was until the car lights were far away. She came out from her hiding place to find the Dikobe family with their arms round each other. Taolo was the first to see her.

"Hey, sis! How is it? So you were hiding here!"

Both Taolo and his father *hugged* Naledi in turn. Rra Dikobe looked terribly tired.

"I'll be going home now, Mma. Shall I take the bandages?"

As Naledi set off with her *flashlight* and the bandages, Taolo ran up beside her.

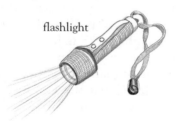

flashlight

"Shouldn't you stay to talk with your mother?"

"Let them be alone together for a while! I won't be long. I'm only walking you home. You know, I missed you."

"What happened to you?" Naledi asked.

He was quiet for a moment, then stopped walking. They were in the dark part of veld separating them from the nearest house.

---

hug, to put one's arms round somebody in greeting

"Compared to some of the others, I had it easy," he said. "They think they can break you. But the opposite is true! Every minute in there, you think about them, and you question, 'What should we have done? What should we do now? What can we do next time?' And when others are with you, you begin to make plans. Even when they try to break you, you go on planning."

Naledi remained quiet while he paused.

"They made me stand for three days and nights on the same spot... but no. I don't feel sorry for myself. They can kill me, and lots of others, but we'll get what we want in the end: to live as free people."

He took her hand as they set off again following the circle of light from the torchlight along the path.

Close to the church, Mma Tshadi's voice coming through the dark took them by surprise, and they let go of each other's hands. Mma Tshadi's large figure appeared behind a flashlight. She had heard and seen the car, and guessed it was something to do with the Dikobes. Happy to hear that both father and son had returned, she told Taolo that she had written to the white magistrate asking to see him with a couple of village elders so they could discuss the removal. As yet there had been no reply. Everyone wanted Saul Dikobe to represent them in the matter of the removal. They were not put off by the banning order and would use Taolo and his mother to carry messages between them. If Rra Dikobe agreed, by tomorrow she would have a *petition* ready that villagers would sign, asking the magistrate to allow them to make him their representative, since their chief had left them. In the meantime, if Rra

petition, a piece of paper signed by many people given or sent to the authorities

Dikobe could outline his plans for resistance to Taolo and his mother, they would hold a meeting to discuss them. Naledi and Taolo offered to help Mma Tshadi take the petition around.

Then Naledi remembered David Sadire. What had happened to him, and why hadn't he been released too? David had been taken away to a hospital, Taolo told her. He had last seen him after David had been returned to his cell following a second *interrogation*. He had been badly tortured and there were burn marks on his body. The boy could not say anything, and it seemed that he had lost his mind. The next day he had been removed from the cell and never returned.

"He was always so quiet! What information could he have?"

"After the first interrogation, he said the police kept asking about Jerry Kau. They were good friends before Jerry left school for the mines."

So the police did suspect that Mma Kau's son had something to do with the fire and the freedom fighters. No wonder Mma Kau was worried. The police had destroyed the quiet David just because he was Jerry's friend. What would they do to Jerry if they caught him?

"Come in the morning!" she said to Taolo. "We can go to Mma Tshadi's together."

---

interrogation, the act of questioning somebody closely and for a long time

Chapter 20

The return of Saul Dikobe and his son brought a new *mood* to Bophelong. People who previously wanted nothing to do with them now saw them as offering their only hope to fight the removal. Within two days, Mma Tshadi's petition was completed and brought to the magistrate's office in the white town together with another letter from Mma Tshadi again asking for an interview with the magistrate.

It surprised Naledi to see how most people in the village were managing to get on with their everyday lives. The fact that the chief was not there to attend to official matters had not yet begun to have an effect, and although the closing of the secondary school was a serious shock, village life continued as if the students were at home on *vacation*. With the recent rains weeds as well as crops were growing, so there was plenty to do in the fields. They all worked hard as usual. They would not accept that the people who had struggled and survived there for all those years should be removed like weeds.

Up at the white farm where she had come to take Nono's place, Naledi pulled at real weeds. Across the beautiful green lawn stood the long fine house with trees round it. Her heart burned with anger at the injustice of it all. A letter had also come from Mma in Jo'burg. The white 'Madam' for whom she worked was not prepared to let her return home at the moment. She would have to wait and ask the 'Madam' again in a week or two.

---

mood [muːd], the state of one's feelings or mind at a particular time
vacation, a period of time when you are not at school or work

84

It was, however, on the day when the authorities refused to pay their *pensions* that the villagers truly realized that their lives had changed forever. Since most of the adults in the village were *pensioners*, who could survive? 5

A week later, Mma Kau and Nono were among those who set out at first light on pension day to make the tiring journey to Boomdal. Naledi *accompanied* her grandmother and stood with her in the long queue, waiting for the office to open. Many pensioners who 10 lived in Boomdal itself were at the head of the queue.

About three hours later the first pensioner reached the desk, only to be turned away and told his money was no longer at that office. It was waiting for him in Bop. The old man stood by the desk, not understand- 15 ing, while an official called for the next person. When the old man did not move, a policeman pulled him aside, telling him to go home. The news went rapidly down the line. The group of people who had been refused their pensions grew all the time, gathering a 20 short distance away from the policeman. Yet each of the remaining villagers continued to wait for his or her turn to reach the desk and hear the words:

"This can only be paid to you in Bophuthatswana. Next!" 25

At last Nono and Naledi were standing before the white official. Naledi stared at him, trying to catch his attention, but his eyes looked right through them. However, before he could shout 'Next!' she interrupt-

---

pension, a sum of money paid regularly by a government to people above a certain age
pensioner, a person receiving a pension
accompany, to go or travel with somebody

85

ed. "How can my grandmother go there? She's ill! Look at her and see for yourself! Where will she get money for food?"

Nono's fingers were pressing hard into her right arm, telling her to calm down.

"Out of the way! Take your grandmother and leave!" the policeman said.

Naledi wanted to scream at him, at the official behind the desk, at the whole lot of them who were working to destroy their lives.

"Are we animals? Why must - "

"Please, Naledi, please, my child... come quietly! Don't make more trouble for us! Let's go home. Come, child!"

Seeing that Nono wasn't feeling well, people in the queue quickly made space for her to sit down. Mma Kau, who had given up her place in the queue, came to help them. Nono refused to go to the hospital. All she needed was a little rest.

Usually, after collecting her money, she would walk to the general store to buy food. But today there was no money and no question of going to the shop. By this time of the month there was hardly any food left at home. Mma sent money every second month, in between the pension payments. How would they manage until then? Most families would be in the same position.

The journey back to Bophelong was made with empty hands. Mma Kau and Naledi, one on each side of Nono, walked in front of the other villagers. When one of the women started to sing quietly, the others gradually joined in. She began with a song about a father who had to leave his family behind in order to look for

86

work in the city. It was a story they all knew too well.

At first Naledi found the singing calmed her. Then she became angry. She wanted to sing songs that could hit out at those who were crushing them. She completed the journey beside Nono in silence. 5

Finally reaching the village, they found Mma Tshadi in the centre of a group of pensioners outside the church. Taolo was sitting to one side on the churchyard wall, listening. Naledi saw his eyes smile at her as she helped Nono sit down to rest. 10

Someone put forward the idea of going into Bop just to collect their money. They would have to pay the bus ticket, but wouldn't that be better than having nothing?

Perhaps it would be *cheaper* to *hire* something like a 15 van or a truck. They had never done anything like this before, but they thought it was a good idea - and they could see no other way to get their money. Looking over to Taolo and Naledi, Mma Tshadi said, "I'm sure these two young people will help. If they go to town 20 tomorrow, they can ask how much it costs."

"Can I, Nono?" Naledi asked.

Nono's face was covered by her hand. Without looking up, she nodded.

"I'll come early," promised Taolo. 25

As soon as they came home, they made a meal with the little food they had left. Then Naledi cleared the table to write a letter to her mother. She kept to the simple facts about the pension and also wrote that their school had been closed. 30

cheap, low in price; costing little money
hire, to obtain the use of something for a short time in return for payment

Turning off the lamp and feeling her way to her sleeping mat, Naledi thought about the next day. She was looking forward to being with Taolo.

Chapter 21

The following morning Taolo came running with news
5 that changed their plans. Three people had arrived from the Anti-Removal Committee and were waiting in the church hall to interview the villagers. While in Johannesburg, his mother had gone to the offices of this organization to tell them about Bophelong. She
10 had kept it a secret even from him, in case the police tried to stop it. Now that members of the committee had arrived, it was important for them to talk to as many people as possible. They needed to gather information about how long each family had been living in
15 Bophelong, what sort of agreements had been made about the land, whether there were any papers and so on. Naledi and Mma Tshadi should go around the village telling people to go to the church. Taolo would go ahead by himself to arrange the transport to collect the
20 pensions.

"My foot is better. I want to go too," Tiro said to his grandmother.

Nono nodded. Could she be changing? wondered Naledi.

25 Entering the church hall, both brother and sister were surprised for the first few moments. Inside, sitting at the table from which Chief Sekete had spoken, were two men and a woman, but the woman and one of the men were white. Almost the only white people who

came to the village were police or government officials.

"These people are from the Anti-Removal Committee and they don't have much time," Mma Dikobe
said. "Can you start by calling Mma Tshadi to meet
them and then work your way around the village? It's
best you don't call Rra Thopi."

"Why is that, Mma?" asked Naledi.

"Someone is informing the police, and he's the only
one who can see our house from where he lives. We're
not certain, but it could be him. So we'll try to keep
him out of this. Of course, if he turns up, we'll just
have to let him in."

The rest of the day was spent carrying messages and
explaining to people why they were needed in the
church hall. Since no one had ever heard of this committee before, Naledi and Tiro found themselves faced
with all sorts of questions to which they had no
answers: How can they help us? Are they friends with
the government? The villagers still came, though, and
were to be further surprised when they saw that two of
the interviewers were white. The white woman, called
Annie, spoke perfect Tswana.

It would have been impossible to keep secret what
was happening inside the church. Apart from the
strange car parked at the back, anyone passing by
could hear the sound of many voices. After their inter-
views, people stayed around discussing the questions
they had been asked. They were also waiting for the
committee to address them and tell them their plans.

At first, Naledi and Tiro called on the villagers who
lived furthest away from Rra Thopi, then Tiro decided
to go by his house and see what he was doing. Running
back to Naledi, he brought the news that they did not

need to worry about Rra Thopi at all. According to his youngest daughter, her father had set off early that morning with his cattle. He was taking them to his brother, who had land about a day's journey away. When Tiro asked the little girl why her father was doing this, she replied, "So they won't be killed when we move to the new place."

That was strange. None of the other villagers who owned cattle had done anything with them yet. People had been saying, quite simply, "How can we move when we have our cattle here?" If Rra Thopi was moving his cattle, perhaps he knew more than the rest of them. Mma Dikobe and the committee would be interested in that.

In the middle of the afternoon, Tiro brought Nono up to the church. She told the white woman when the family had first come to Bophelong and what their present circumstances were. The story Nono told was one the children knew well - how their father's father saved the life of Chief Sekete's father during the Second World War. After the war, Chief Sekete's father offered their grandfather a piece of land on which to build a house, as well as some cattle. It was land that the Sekete family had bought many years earlier, before the law that stopped black people from buying land in most places. While Chief Sekete's father and their grandfather were alive, their family never had to pay rent. But after both the old men died, the present chief began to ask their father to pay, saying that he needed money for his growing family. There were no papers to show that their grandfather had been given the land.

Nono felt in her pocket. She had a little card, which she had kept carefully. It had been given to her hus-

90

band when he left the army. Nono handed the old
paper to the white woman. It was from the Prime Minister of the day and had a 'V' at the top:

V

WELCOME 5

HOME!

I wish you a very hearty welcome home, after
your long *absence*. I hope you enjoy your stay
in the future country and are ready for the
work that lies ahead, wherever it may be. 10

J. Smuts

The white woman looked at the letter. Nono continued her story, telling how her husband, who had
developed back problems during the war, was unable to
get any *compensation* when he could no longer work 15
because of the pain. She had supported the family herself with her small earnings from working on local
white farms and the few crops they grew for themselves
at Bophelong. Money problems had forced them to sell
their animals after her husband's death. 20

When her son was sixteen, he went to work in the
mines and sent home a little money each month. After
he married, his wife earned money working for a white
family in the city, so Nono had brought up her son's
children. Then her son had died from the '*coughing* 25
sickness', which he caught in the mines. Since then,
she and the children had lived on her small pension -
which she had been refused yesterday - and the money

---

absence, a state of being away
compensation, something, especially an amount of money, given to
balance or reduce the bad effect of damage or loss, etc
coughing ['kɒfɪŋ] *sickness*, bad health from *coughing*, see picture, page 92

the man
coughs

the children's mother sent from Jo'burg. When she had finished her story, Tiro helped her home.

By the end of the day, there were still a few people who had not been interviewed. Nor had there been any time for a general discussion. Joe, the black man on the committee, and his two white companions said they would continue the following day.

Mma Tshadi told the three they could sleep in her house. Annie thanked Mma Tshadi warmly, admitting they would be in trouble without the help of the people they visited.

The sun was sinking as Naledi and Tiro hurried home. Taolo had not yet returned and Naledi was beginning to worry about him. Might he have gone looking for some of his friends? Or had the police already found them?

Chapter 22

Taolo was talking to Joe at the back of the church hall when Naledi and Tiro arrived in the morning. A couple of children at the water tap had already told Naledi they had seen him.

He glanced towards the door as she entered, giving

a slight nod, then continued talking. Nearby, sitting in a circle in deep conversation, were Mma Dikobe, Mma Tshadi, the two white people and a man with his back to the door. As she moved into the hall, Naledi recognized him. It was Rev. Radebe! At the same moment, 5 Mma Dikobe glanced at her watch. "My goodness! It will be time for the service soon. Come here, Naledi!"

Of course, it was Sunday! Naledi had completely forgotten. Nono had remained in bed, still very tired from the trip to Boomdal. Normally she would never 10 miss a Sunday service.

Mma Dikobe took Naledi's hand and said to Rev. Radebe, "Reverend, this child was one of those elected to represent the students at the secondary school. I'm sure she would be pleased to hear about some of 15 her friends."

Rev. Radebe got up from his seat and took Naledi's free hand in both of his. "I expect that you know from Mma Dikobe that your friend Theresa is still in a very bad state. But for the moment your other friends on 20 the committee are alright. They're trying to lie low until things are quieter, but I hear they've been very busy!" He smiled. "The latest news is that there is now a Boomdal *Youth* Association - the B.Y.A. - and your friends intend organizing the young people to join with 25 our Resistance Committee."

"Can you get a message to them, Rra? We need to meet them."

"I don't think you need me. You'll find your friend Taolo managed to see them yesterday. But now, excuse 30 me. I must get ready for the service."

| *youth*, the time when a person is young

93

Taolo came up to Naledi. "Take a seat." They sat at the far end where they could talk quietly. He had managed to see Zach, Dan and Ben. Although they were still in hiding, they were planning a meeting where they would decide what to do next. When the place and date were decided, someone would come to Bophelong to let them know. Taolo had been to the white town to arrange transport into Bop on Monday for the pensions. It was expensive, so he had then had to go back into Boomdal to ask for Rev. Radebe's help with the money. Every pensioner would have to pay ten rand to hire a truck. When the owner had asked about the reason for the trip, Taolo had just told him that the villagers wanted to see the place where they were being moved to. Taolo had been surprised to discover that not all the town's white people were in favour of the removal. Many of the shopkeepers would lose customers, since Boomdal people often shopped in the white town where many of them worked. He laughed.

"When it comes to money, there's no colour problem for them!"

Rev. Radebe's voice interrupted them. "Welcome, my brothers and sisters, in this difficult time. Today we have some special visitors."

The service was about to begin. Rev. Radebe used words and hymns to carry extra meaning. As they sang and Naledi let her voice and heart fly up - as if free for a few moments - she felt sorry that she hadn't brought Nono.

Immediately after the service the three visitors addressed the *congregation*. Joe did most of the talking.

---

congregation, a group of people gathered together in a church to hear the religious service

94

"My friends, we can't tell you what you should do. But we can tell you how others have tried to resist and what methods they used. Every place is different, but one thing is certain. The only way to stay where you are is to stay completely united!   5

"The first thing the authorities always do is to make divisions among you. They will offer one person something, another one something else, *put pressure on* the next - and before you know it, people will be going. That makes it impossible for those who want to stay."   10

Explaining which laws would be used to move the people of Bophelong and Boomdal, Joe said that he believed the government would act against the villagers first because they were regarded as 'squatters'. Only the Sekete family would get anything for their land.   15 Probably the villagers' only hope was to get their story into the newspapers, because the government did not like people from other countries hearing about removals. Indeed, the Minister of 'Cooperation and Development' had stated to the world that no one in   20 South Africa was forced to move to a 'homeland'. Everyone chose to go!

A long discussion followed. It was decided that Mma Tshadi should not wait any longer for a reply from the magistrate but go to his office herself the next day and 25 demand an interview. Taolo was to accompany her. If the magistrate refused to let Rra Dikobe represent them (which seemed likely), then at least he should let them appoint someone else they trusted. In the meantime Mma Tshadi and the Dikobes would draw up two let-   30

---

put pressure on somebody, to force or try to force somebody to do something

95

ters - one to be sent to the Minister and the other to a national newspaper, so many people would hear about their problem.

The rest of the day passed quickly. In the afternoon they watched the car with Joe and his friends disappear across the veld. Naledi was very hungry and Mma Dikobe told her to come and take some food from her.

On the way to the Dikobes' house they noticed that Rra Thopi had returned from his cattle journey. He was outside his house watching them. Had he arrived back in time to see the car leaving the church, or had his children said anything to him?

That evening they made plans for the following morning. Tiro would accompany Nono in the truck to Bop, while Naledi would go to the farm again to do Nono's work. Dineo would have to come with her, as Mma Kau would also be away collecting her pension. Tomorrow was going to be a busy day for everyone. The village would be left almost empty, apart from Saul and a few boys minding the animals.

Chapter 23

No one was prepared for the sight that met them on their return to the village late the following afternoon. Naledi heard an engine as she walked past the fields and Rra Thopi's empty cattle *enclosure* on her way back from the white farm. Perhaps it was the hired truck. Naledi tried to speed up, but it had been a long, hard day, and the child on her back slowed her down.

enclosure, a piece of land with a fence around

96

As the path rose up a small hill, the centre of the village came into view. Where was the church? There were only two broken walls with no roof and with big holes for windows. Where Taolo had been standing at the back of the hall the day before, there was nothing, just a lot of *rubble*. A short distance away stood an enormous yellow *bulldozer*. The pensioners who had just climbed out of their large truck stared at it.

Naledi forgot that she was tired and ran. Nono was sitting on some stones with tears in her eyes. Then Rra Rampou slowly picked up a stone and put it in place on the broken wall. Then he went back and collected the next stone.

bulldozer

rubble

A woman called out, "We shall build it up again!" She joined the old man and immediately others began to follow suit.

Rra Thopi was the first of the villagers who worked in Boomdal to return, riding his new bicycle. "What's this?" he called out.

"Do your eyes not see?" replied Rra Rampou.

When it became dark it was decided that whoever was able would continue the work the next day. As they left to go home, they heard Mma Tshadi calling to them. She and Taolo were returning from their visit to the magistrate.

They reported that magistrate had kept them waiting the whole day before agreeing to see them. There had been nowhere to sit and they had been left standing in the *corridor*, since the waiting room was for 'Whites Only'. Finally they had been allowed into the magistrate's room. He continued writing at his desk for a time before looking up at them. He asked Mma Tshadi why she was causing him trouble when "everything should be quite clear by now to you people." When she asked for his reply to the villagers' *request* that Saul Dikobe represent them, the magistrate became very angry. He shouted at them that Chief Sekete was still their chief - and would remain so until he died, and the sooner they all went to join him in Bop, the better. Then he had warned Taolo, saying that he knew all about his activities and how foolish he was to follow in his father's footsteps. Without allowing them any discussion, the magistrate had them shown out.

corridor, a long narrow way through a house from which doors open into rooms
request, an act of politely asking for something

Mma Tshadi's account shocked everyone. How could they win against an enemy like the magistrate?

"What can we do?" The speaker voiced everyone's feelings.

"My friends, it's not finished yet! We must prepare 5 for a long struggle." It was Mma Dikobe's voice. She must have arrived while Mma Tshadi was speaking. "Why should you be surprised at the magistrate? Has he not always behaved in this way to you? Should we give up now because of this man? No... we have a plan. 10 Already we are busy with a letter to the Minister as our friends from the Removal Committee advised. We'll tell him we are being forced out against our wishes and he said no one is to be forced."

Her voice was soft, yet clear. "He too will not pay 15 any attention to our letter unless he sees that many people are watching him. So we will ask our friends to give a copy of our letter to the newspapers. They can photograph our ruined church and send these pictures all around the country, even to other countries. But we 20 must speak with **one** voice. If some of us give in, then they will break us off one by one."

The moon rose into the night sky. Before leaving, they agreed to hold a meeting to elect their own village committee to represent them in the trouble 25 ahead, no matter what the magistrate had said. Why should they let their enemy decide their future?

Chapter 24

At home Naledi hurried to prepare some of the food
Nono had bought after collecting her pension money.
The shop prices in Bop had been even higher than in
Boomdal. Speaking to local customers, the villagers
were told that most of the shops were owned by people
who were friendly to those in high places. It seemed
that to get on in that place you not only had to be
Tswana, you had to belong to the president's party.

It was late when they finished eating. Usually by
this time they would be fast asleep. But when Naledi
asked Nono if she could go for a short while to Mma
Dikobe's to see how the letter was coming on, her
grandmother did not object. Was Nono just too worn
out to worry any longer, or was this another sign of a
change of heart? She nodded when Tiro announced
that he would go as well.

On their way in the dark, they noticed that there
was still light in one of Rra Thopi's rooms. His was the
only house from which the Dikobes could be seen. In
fact, one of his windows faced their house. Glancing at
it, Naledi thought she saw a movement at the curtain.

The Dikobes' house was also still lit up. Naledi
knocked at the door and called softly, "It's only us!"

Mma Dikobe opened and let them in quickly. At the
table sat Taolo with Mma Tshadi and Rra Rampou.
There was a seat for Mma Dikobe and an extra one
pushed aside, as if someone else had gotten up in a hurry.

"We came to see you about the letter," Tiro said.

With one of her rare slow smiles, Mma Tshadi put
her hand down the front of her dress and produced a
piece of paper that she placed on the table.

100

At the same time, a door opened behind her and Saul Dikobe came in and sat down at the table. "Look, Lydia, if they want to take me, they'll take me. We're just too short of time to play their games. We must get the letter finished tonight. Let's continue now. It's 5 almost done."

Rra Dikobe passed Naledi the letter. "Read it to us," he said. "Then we can all hear how it sounds."

Naledi looked down at the letter. It was written in English. 10

"Sir, we have heard that a statement has been made that there will be no more forced removals. Only those who want to go will be moved. So we wish to bring our position to your *urgent* attention.

"Bophelong is *freehold* land that has been owned by 15 members of the Sekete family since 1910. A *Deed* of Transfer is held by Mr Elias Sekete, who was our chief until he deserted us nearly four weeks ago. The farm was bought before the law was passed forbidding black people to own land here. In fact, some of the families 20 were already living together in this place before 1910. We find that Elias Sekete, who was our chief, has agreed for all of us to move to the place called Bophu-thatswana. When the truth came out and he saw how angry the people were, he ran away. We do not believe 25 he can represent us anymore. This is why we are appointing a Bophelong Village Committee to speak with one voice for all of us.

"Many of us have our own *plots* for growing crops.

urgent ['ɜːdʒənt], that cannot wait
freehold, complete ownership of property
deed, (law) a signed agreement, especially about legal rights
plot, a piece of land

This land adds to our income and has helped to keep some of us from starving in hard times. There is also common land here for grazing our cattle. We hear that in Bophuthatswana only the landowners will receive land for growing and grazing. We can not have any land. What would happen then to our cattle? How will we manage without cattle and without land?

"Over the years we have constructed a fine stone building for our church. This week, without any warning, our church was destroyed by men on government trucks.

"Children with parents who can afford it walk daily to school in Boomdal, where there is a Primary and Secondary school. Our community paid to help build these two schools.

"Many of our younger people are working in town or away from the district, but the women and girls can get work on neighbouring farms. In Bophuthatswana the only work available is far away and transport costs are high.

"The people of Bophelong are totally against this removal."

Naledi's voice came to a halt where the letter stopped.

"What do you think of it?" asked Rra Dikobe.

"What you write is all true, but why should this Minister listen? It's **his** people that want to force us away!"

"That's why we don't send it only to him. We will make copies and get it published to bring it out into the open as quickly as possible," Taolo said.

"That's why poor people like us need to join together like a *chain*, so that together we can be strong." Taolo's father said.

chain

Mma Dikobe told them the letter had to be finished. They worked on it for a while. Then Mma Dikobe sent the children home.

There was still a light in one of the rooms of Rra Thopi's house.   5

Chapter 25

Early the next morning there was a loud knocking at the door. Struggling up from her mat, Naledi pulled on her dress. Nono lay in bed, still very tired from the previous day's journey.

Outside were two of the Sadire children with the   10
news that no water was coming from the tap. What should they do? Their mother was at work and their little brother was not well and needed water. Naledi gave them a cupful of the little water they still had.

Tiro and Dineo set off at a run towards the tap. As   15
Naledi approached, she could see Mma Tshadi and Tao-lo among the small crowd. People could not believe there was no water. Why should the water stop so suddenly? Every month their chief used to collect money from each family to pay to the white farmer who owned   20
the *dam*. No one knew what had happened since Rra

dam, see picture, page 104

dam

Sekete had left them, but surely the farmer would not just cut them off? Why had he not sent someone to the village to ask for the money if that was the problem?

Someone would have to go to the farmer to find out the reason. Someone else could begin to collect money, and those at work would be asked to pay at the meeting planned for the evening.

It was quite a distance to the farm. Mma Tshadi asked Taolo and Naledi to hurry over there. They cut across the grazing veld behind the Dikobes' house. There was no path. The quickest way to the dam was simply to follow the line of piping that carried the water to the village tap.

When they came close to the farm, a voice brought them to a halt. Coming up behind them from the direction of the dam was a man. His manner was not unfriendly, but he wanted to know what the young people were doing so close to the farm. He was the 'boss-boy', and he had to report to the farmer on all comings and goings.

"We're from Bophelong, Rra. There's no water," Naledi told him.

"People want to know what's happened, so we've come to see the farmer," Taolo added.

It was a bad thing, the man said. But the water had indeed been cut off late the previous evening, following a visit by the police. Police and soldiers often came to the farm these days. It was all this business of what they called 'terrorists'." 5

"But why did the farmer stop our water?"

"The police say the terrorists are in your village. That's why they told my boss he must stop the water."

Suddenly it was quite clear. It was not the money at all. First the church was destroyed. Now the water. 10 The farmer was simply helping the authorities to force them away. It seemed there was nothing they could do.

The journey back felt much longer. They were both hot and *thirsty*. The attack was coming from all sides. How would they manage without the tap? By carrying 15 buckets all the way on foot from Boomdal?

As they came in sight of Taolo's house, they saw a grey Land- Rover*, coming to a stop outside the Dikobe house. A group of figures could be seen jumping out of the back and running up the path. 20

With a shout, Taolo ran forward. Naledi shouted, "Wait, Taolo! Maybe it's you they're looking for!"

But he didn't slow down until they saw the same figures returning to the Land-Rover and jumping into the back again. They were close enough now to see that a 25 couple of them wore army caps, although the rest of their clothes were ordinary. The two men in front of the car were white, those behind them were black. Suddenly the Land-Rover left the path and came

---

thirsty ['θɜːstɪ], feeling thirst, that is the need for something to drink
*a strong motor car

quickly across the veld. It was heading straight towards them.

There was nowhere to go. In no time at all the Land-Rover was right in front of them. Four large men jumped out, took Taolo and pulled him into the back.

Chapter 26

A few moments later, Rra Dikobe reached Naledi. When the men had come into the house and had pushed him away, he knew they were after Taolo. But there had been no way to warn him. Everything had happened so quickly.

"They could take him anywhere, and there's almost nothing we can do."

Should she go to the hospital and tell Mma Dikobe? But Rra Dikobe said she must find Rev. Radebe first. If he picked up Mma Dikobe in his car, together they might be able to start a search. Naledi quickly told him about the water, then hurried off to find Mma Tshadi. They had to get water from Boomdal as soon as possible. They needed Rev. Radebe's help in both matters.

It took Naledi and Tiro over an hour to find Rev. Radebe, but once found, he rapidly moved into action in his old blue Ford. Within a short time he not only got them six large *barrels* of water, but also told an old friend to make the journey in his van to Bophelong with the water and the two young people. They would come with water every day. He would take care of that. He promised to pick up Mma Dikobe from the hospital, and together they would look for Taolo in the immediate area.

barrel

****

That evening the villagers met beside the *piles* of stones
in the church yard. A table and a chair had been produced from somewhere. Everyone knew about the
attack on Taolo. Naledi had to keep fighting off an
image of a figure lying motionless, hidden in the long
grass. She wondered what Taolo's father must be going
through, alone in his house. At the same time, her eyes
followed the movements of Rra Thopi. For a while he
stood near Mma Tshadi and Rra Rampou. Now he
moved to the back, quite close to where she stood. He
was looking sideways, over in the direction of Boomdal.

Then Rev. Radebe arrived with Mma Dikobe.

"My friends, while we are gathered this evening, in
this place that others have deserted, another one of
our children is missing…"

When the prayer was over, the discussion turned to

pile, a number of things lying one on top of another

107

the reason for the meeting. Mma Dikobe began to read the letter. When she came to the end of it and the final words, 'For these reasons, we are not prepared to move,' there was a silence and then *applause*.

5 Suddenly, two figures came towards the table. Shocked cries greeted Saul Dikobe as he entered the ring of light carrying Taolo on his shoulder.

"Bring him to the car. Let me take him to the hospital," Rev. Radebe said.

10 "First... the meeting!" Taolo's words cut across the gathering.

"He told me to bring him here... came back from where they left him... wouldn't stay at home..."

Carefully he put Taolo on the chair. The right side
15 of Taolo's face was cut, his right eye almost closed. But

applause [ə'plɔːz], to clap your hands in praise

108

he would not go to the hospital until after the meeting.

It was Tiro who noticed Rra Thopi leaving. Tiro told Mma Tshadi and within seconds the message had been passed on. Mma Dikobe told her husband to leave the gathering. The disappearance of Rra Thopi could only mean one thing.

Everyone was quiet; all eyes looked at the family around the table.

"No!" Rra Dikobe said. "They are **not** going to make me run like a frightened dog! I will **not** leave my son so they can attack him all over again! No, they are **not** going to stop me from talking here tonight! Will they destroy me, my family, my people while I must sit quietly by and watch? Oh no!"

His deep voice rang out into the dark night. Perhaps Rra Thopi could hear him too... or whoever was listening out there. Naledi felt the whole world could have been listening and Saul Dikobe would still have spoken the exact same words. He spoke of those with power who used it to break the weak, of the white authorities pushing them off their land.

He spoke of those from their own community who helped the authorities, but they would not be safe from people's anger. Had their own chief's house not been set on fire?

And then he began to speak of resistance, especially of the spirit of young people who were saying, 'No' when their parents were not yet sure about what to do. This time they were determined to fight it out to the end. Many times in the past people had joined to resist the unjust laws. They had formed unions. Almost thirty years ago, as a young man in his early twenties, he had made his way to a place called Kliptown, where

109

people from all across the country, from all backgrounds, had come to agree on a *Freedom Charter*. Although the government kept trying to crush and destroy them, it could never put out the fire in people's
5 hearts, their burning *desire* for freedom.

He continued speaking even when two cars appeared from the direction of Boomdal.

"You must elect your committee. When the police come for some of them, you'll find new people to take
10 their places, old and young."

When the two cars came to a halt right beside them, Saul Dikobe was still speaking. He continued even as uniformed men jumped out shining their flashlights.

"Saul Dikobe!" a voice said.

15 Slowly Rra Dikobe turned his head toward the light.

"This meeting is *illegal*. You had better tell your little gathering to go home."

No one moved. The voice spoke in English. Another one followed, this time in Tswana.

20 "Go to your homes! This meeting is illegal!"

Rev. Radebe was the first to answer, moving toward the first voice. "I'm a priest. Let me talk to the one in charge."

"There's nothing to discuss. Everyone must go
25 home... except Saul Dikobe. He's coming with us."

With that, bodies and flashlights suddenly came forward toward Saul. Naledi heard Taolo shout.

"Leave him!"

There was the sound of a shot and screams...

Freedom Charter, the power or right to act, speak, etc according to a written statement by a government
desire [dɪ'zaɪə], very strong wish
illegal, not legal

110

"Oh God! Oh God! They've killed him!" Mma Dikobe cried.

The yellow lamp was knocked off the table. The white light from the flashlights cut through the dark. At the end of one of them lay the body of Saul Dikobe. 5

Chapter 27

Naledi was lying on her mat but she could not sleep. She kept seeing Rra Dikobe lying dead on the ground. Rev. Radebe had argued with the police over the body, trying to stop them from taking it away. The police were shouting that everybody should go home. With 10 their rifles they were forcing people away from the church yard. Children were screaming and Dineo was lost in the crush. The villagers watched Rra Dikobe's body being lifted into one of the cars and driven off towards Boomdal. Then Rev. Radebe left, taking with 15 him Mma Dikobe and Taolo.

Dineo was screaming in the room next door. There was nothing Nono could do to make her stop. Naledi took her from Nono's bed. Sitting by the table in the dark with the little body in her arms, Naledi knew how 20 unprotected her sister was. Tiro, at eleven, had his own way of hating those with power over them. As they returned home that night, his young face had been hard. Naledi knew how much he respected Rra Dikobe. He had loved their own father so much. He had been 25 killed by the sickness from the white people's mines. Her brother had changed since then, and now that the guns had taken away Rra Dikobe, he was not going to

111

let his pain show, perhaps not even to himself. It was too big.

Naledi could not stop her tears. They were hot and angry.

You had to go on. Mma Dikobe and Taolo had to go on. Her friend Grace, whether she was in hiding or in prison, had to go on. Their own Mma had to go on. They all had to continue in their different ways.

There was a terrible noise. They were the same sounds as the evening before but now with a new sound added. A voice was shouting over a megaphone. They were being told to move!...

"Pack all your *belongings*. Put them outside. Take down any parts of your house you want to go with you. Don't leave your yard without permission until you're told to put things onto the trucks."

Opening the door just enough to look outside, Naledi and Tiro saw flashlights in all directions. Behind them was a row of trucks and buses. The noise was coming from the direction of Mma Tshadi's place. They could not see her house, but soon a group of figures were going toward the trucks. Someone was being pushed along the path. Naledi understood who it was. The police could control Mma Tshadi's body, but not her voice. Was she being taken to Bop or to prison?

Then Naledi and Tiro saw a couple of people coming in their direction. They shut the door. Then someone knocked on it.

"Open up! Open up!"

Neither Naledi nor Tiro moved. Seconds later there was the sound of glass breaking and lights shone into

| *belongings*, that which a person owns (not land and houses)

the room. Dineo was running across the room, screaming to get to her sister. From Nono's bed came a whisper, "Oh, God! What now?"

Then the light from a flashlight caught Naledi right
in the eyes.   5

"Why did you not open the door? Hurry up!"

Two large men pushed inside. One of them said to
Nono, "Why are you not up old woman? Today is
moving day. You must get up and get everything ready."

When Nono made no reply, the policeman turned   10
to Naledi. "What's wrong with her?"

"Our grandmother is sick. You can see for yourself.
How can she get up?"

"You'll have to make the place ready yourselves
then. If you don't put your belongings outside, they'll   15
be broken up with the house. Sick or not sick, everyone is moving from here today. We'll be back soon."

What could they do? There was no time to think
clearly or to plan. If they did not take their furniture
and other things out of the house for removal, every-   20
thing would be destroyed as the bulldozer moved in.

Although Tiro had not said a word since the police
had broken in, he began to help Naledi put things outside. By the time *dawn* came, everything was in a small
pile in front of the house.   25

Across the village similar things were going on. The
work of a lifetime was reduced to a few small piles of
furniture. What about the vegetables in the fields?
Were they supposed to leave them behind? The hens
were put inside boxes. It seemed that only animals and   30
young children had the energy to give voice to their

dawn, the time of the day when the first light appears

113

protests. Everyone else was silent. What happened yesterday evening was still fresh in their minds.

Chapter 28

As dawn turned to morning, the bulldozer began its attack. The villagers watched as the chain of com-
5 mand took effect. First, three white policemen climbed down from one of the trucks and a message was passed to the groups of black policemen standing in front of their cars. Two of them marched to a truck further back. They opened the door and a dozen or so black
10 men in blue overalls jumped down. One went across to the bulldozer. It was these men who were to carry out the work under the sharp eyes of the police.

As the bulldozer began its approach, people broke the silence and shouts filled the air.
15 "God will punish you!"

But the machine still went forward. Could these men imagine their own homes, parents, wives and children being destroyed? If they could, they did not show it. But they did not look into the eyes of the villagers.
20 Whose house would they destroy first? A policeman was pointing at Rra Rampou's stone *cottage*. The bull-dozer went across towards it. It was the one that Rra Rampou had worked on for years, slowly buying and placing a few more stones each month, determined to
25 complete a house that could last for a hundred years.

"I want my children's children and their children to remember me!" he used to say.

| *cottage* ['kɒtɪdʒ], a small house

114

Although it was difficult to get a good view from Nono's yard, Naledi could see no sign of Rra Rampou. The door of the house, with its white-painted number, was closed, and there seemed to be no pile outside the house. 5

"Rra Rampou must be inside! He hasn't brought anything out!" Mma Kau shouted to Naledi.

"He'll die in there!" Tiro said.

"But they have to stop! Someone must get him out!" Naledi ran towards the bulldozer. Nono was calling 10 her to come back. But she had to stop the machine; she had to! She ran forward, almost reaching the bull-dozer. Surely the driver would not push in the walls when he knew an old man was inside? She cried out to him, "Stop, Rra! You must stop ..." 15

A hand took hold of her arm.

"Did you not hear the order? Why are you not in your yard?" A policeman's thick fingers were crushing her arm.

"There's an old man... in the house... You'll kill him ..." 20

"You think we're stupid? We know he'll run out. Old people are full of talk! Now get back to your place. Your house is next."

The policeman pushed her backward. But the driv-er had stopped the bulldozer. He obviously understood 25 her, even though he spoke to the policeman in a lan-guage that was not Tswana.

By now other policemen, including one of the white men, had come forward. Then they stormed the cot-tage with their rifles. They broke the windows. The 30 white officer was the first to climb through. Shortly afterwards, the door opened and they marched out with Rra Rampou between them.

Then they signalled to the workers in *overalls* and ordered them to clear out the old man's belongings. They could have five minutes to throw everything outside before the bulldozer driver got to work.

5 As Rra Rampou's house came falling down, the first of the white farmers arrived with their cattle trucks. They had heard of the removal and were coming to see what animals could be bought cheaply.

Shortly afterwards, another message came over the 10 megaphone. "Only pigs and hens can be transported. If you still have cattle, you have a last chance to sell them now. Those who have cattle may leave their yards to come and talk with the farmers here."

Naledi immediately thought of Rra Thopi. His cat- 15 tle were all safely out of the way. So he was not among the men and women who now came forward. The farmers were offering very low prices and the villagers had to accept. What else could they do?

The bulldozer began to make its way along the track 20 in their direction. Seeing the machine approaching them, Dineo buried her face in Nono's arms. Naledi pushed her hand into her mouth to stop herself shouting as the bulldozer hit the yard's mud wall. She and Tiro had helped Mma build that wall on one of her vis- 25 its. Now they saw it break in a thousand places...

The driver drove straight ahead and hit their house. How could one person help break down another's home? Naledi felt angry and hurt. The pain rose up with each movement of the machine.

30 Dry-eyed, she watched their home reduced to a pile

| *overalls*, loose, strong clothing worn over clothes to protect them

116

of rubble before the bulldozer went on to the next house. It pushed its way onward across the village, across carefully tended vegetable gardens, fences and walls, whatever lay in its way.

Slowly the lorries began filling up as people were forced, under the eyes of the armed police, to put their goods onto them with the help of the men in blue overalls.

Nono sat wordlessly on the earth that had been her home since the time she had become a young married woman. Now she closed her eyes, for she did not want to see anymore. Naledi kneeled down beside her, taking her hand. It felt cold. Her grandmother's energy seemed to be slipping away, here in the place where she had looked after and cared for her children and grand-children.

"Please, Nono, please don't give up now," Naledi whispered. "We'll come back. It's not finished, Nono, it's not finished."

Slowly the lorry went off. All around they saw houses without roofs, doors, windows... broken walls... piles of rubble...

Naledi remembered Saul Dikobe and his words, "No! They are **not** going to make me run like a frightened dog." And Taolo's words the night he had come out of prison and walked home with her, taking her hand. "They can kill me, and lots of others, but we will get what we want in the end, to live like free people."

Chapter 29

Lying on her mat among her possessions, on the night of their arrival in the *camp*, Naledi couldn't sleep. Even with the two windows wide open, the hot air remained inside the small box, their new 'home'.

5   It had been late afternoon before they and their pile of belongings had been dumped outside an iron *hut*, simply one of hundreds set in long rows on the hard, dry earth of Matlapeng. The name suited it, 'place of stones'. For some families there were not even huts. It 10 was in the middle of nowhere... and while Bophelong had been full of life, this place seemed fit only for death.

Mma Kau was in the iron hut next to them. Although they had always been neighbours within 15 calling distance, there had always been veld between them. Now they were practically within whispering distance. Tiro had been sent out for water and Naledi was making a small fire outside over which to cook. Mma Kau had helped to settle Nono. For how much 20 longer would she be like this? Nono's health was very poor and Naledi wondered how she would get along without Mma Dikobe's help. In addition, the pills would soon run out.

Two days later Joe arrived from the Anti-Removal 25 Committee with a friend who worked on a newspaper. Rev. Radebe had telephoned to tell him the bad news. Reaching the camp early in the morning, the two men

camp, a place where people are kept in *huts* especially by a goverment and often for long periods
hut, a small simply built house, usually made of wood or mud

118

were anxious to get away before their presence was reported to the police. Joe took photographs: the lines of huts without fields, the rock-hard *landscape* that made farming impossible. He photographed Mma Tshadi standing outside her new hut and Rra Rampou leaning on his stick, his eyes fixed on the horizon in the direction of the home from which he had been taken. As people spoke, the reporter wrote busily in his notebook. Mma Tshadi said they would never stop demanding to be taken back to Bophelong. How were people meant to live here?

"Only God knows why He let us be taken from our land. But one day He will punish those who throw us, His children, around like stones," said Rra Rampou.

"But we can't wait so long, Rra. We must do something ourselves." Naledi watched the reporter put down her words.

Then Joe and his friend were gone and they were left with the empty feeling of being completely cut off again. Only the fittest were meant to survive here. Only those with work outside this huge prison called a 'homeland' - and with money to pay the expensive bus ticket - could leave.

No one was really surprised when it was discovered that Rra Thopi had not been moved along with them to the same place. He had been taken to the place where the Sekete family lived, on the other side of some low hills.

Although she was weak and dependent on Naledi and Tiro, Nono still asked them daily about school.

---

landscape, all the features of an area which can be seen when looking across it

Where was it? Nono was talking more and more about the past. In fact, she seemed hardly able to take in their new surroundings.

There was only a *makeshift* primary school at Matla-peng and no secondary school. For a long time the authorities had been promising to build a proper primary shool, but in the meantime children were being taught in a house built by the people themselves. Naledi and Tiro went up close to look through an open door. The room was full of children. A tired teacher sat on the only chair in the room.

"I'm not going there!" protested Tiro.

"Where else can you go?" asked Naledi.

The nearest secondary school was far away. Students travelled to it by bus because it was in another area and too far to walk, so it would be necessary to have money for the bus ticket too. The school year was coming to an end and a new one would begin in a couple of months. Someone told Naledi that the students there had also been protesting. There had also been some expulsions.

But before any decisions could be made about schooling, they needed to hear from Mma. Naledi wrote to her the day after their removal. Her reply would have to be collected from the post office in the local shop. It was one of the few mud-walled buildings set among the iron huts. Like the tap, it was a place for people to meet and talk. Every day, following the usual trip to collect water, Naledi went to the shop to ask if there was a letter for her.

After more than a week it came.

| *makeshift*, used to serve for a while as the real thing is not there

'I was praying this would not happen. I am sending you the newspaper where I saw all the bad news. I can't believe our home is gone. I hope to come and see you very soon.'

Mma's employer was planning to go away on vacation for two weeks over Christmas, so she would come then. The newspaper had a picture of Rra Rampou standing outside an iron hut. Next to it was a report about the removal. 'BLACK SPOT' REMOVED: 'THEY THROW US AROUND LIKE STONES'. Slowly she read through the English words. Then she saw another, smaller report below.

'FIGHT FOR BODY CONTINUES'

'The wife of the dead trade union leader, Saul Dikobe, is still trying to *recover* the body of her husband from the police.

Mr Dikobe, a banned person, was shot dead earlier this week during a meeting to voice protest against the plans to bulldoze homes and remove residents of Bophelong to the homeland Bophuthatswana. Mr Dikobe was banished to Bophelong earlier this year after completing a ten-year prison sentence on Robben Island.

It is thought that police may be holding back the body so it cannot be buried in Soweto on the weekend, when a large crowd would be expected to attend.'

The report did not say where Mma Dikobe was, nor anything about Taolo, but it mentioned Soweto, which had been the family's home before. It was almost certain Mma Dikobe and Taolo would return to live there again.

recover, here, to get back

121

Naledi stood in the sun, the paper in her hand, looking across the landscape of dried earth and iron huts. She was missing Taolo so badly, more now than when he had been in prison. It was foolish to dream of
5 how good it would be if they could be together.

Chapter 30

Two weeks before Christmas, Rev. Radebe arrived unexpectedly. Many people came to hear him in front of Mma Tshadi's hut. As ever, Rev. Radebe's words seemed to carry special meaning. "Christmas is a time
10 of hope, especially for those who are suffering...."

Mma would be coming any day now, but this Christmas there would be no *celebrations*. She was going to be shocked to see Nono's condition. Mma Kau helped the children constantly, but their grandmother's energy
15 was quickly disappearing.

Chief Sekete had come over to the camp full of smiles and greetings, expressing his happiness to be back with 'his people'. He had used his old fatherly tone to Naledi, saying she should come and see Poleng
20 before his daughter left for boarding school. Angry, Naledi turned away. So Poleng was there, but she had not come.

"Christmas is a time for new beginnings. Children of Bophelong, it is time for you to elect those who should
25 represent you in your just struggle to return to your true homes."

Was Rev. Radebe helping with another election?

| *celebrations*, a way of marking a happy or important day

122

People were putting up their hands in support of Mma Tshadi, Rra Rampou and others. Then Mma Tshadi proposed her, Naledi, as a youth member. Hands and voices elected her too. They chose Rra Rampou to be their new chief. He was the only one they would trust, along with the committee they now elected.

Tiro pulled at Naledi's arm.

"The Reverend is calling you!"

Naledi made her way through to the front. Rev. Radebe led her a short way aside from the gathering.

"I have something for you. I promised especially to see this would reach you safely." He gave her a letter. "Mma Dikobe was in Boomdal a few days ago to collect the things I brought from their house. She wanted very much to see you and your family but there was no time. She had to get back to work. She said she would miss you greatly, but would try to keep in touch. She's going to help the Anti-Removal committee. They are planning a special campaign on Bophelong."

Naledi's heart was beating fast. There was so much she wanted to know. Perhaps it would be in the letter.

"By the way, will you show me your house after I'm finished here? I want to see your grandmother. Mma Dikobe told me about her illness." He turned and made his way back to his congregation.

Wanting to read her letter undisturbed, Naledi walked away in the opposite direction. In Bophelong she could easily have found a quiet place in the veld. But here there were only iron huts. She opened the letter and pulled out a photograph cut out from a newspaper. It showed an enormous crowd of marching people. Her eyes went to the bottom of the page. The letter was not from Mma Dikobe after all. It was from Taolo.

Dear Sis Naledi,

So much has been happening that I haven't had time to write. We heard that you were forced to move the day after Rra was killed. Please write and tell me
5 how it is where you are. You can get my address from the friend who brings this letter.

We had a hard time getting my father's body. We buried him on Wednesday and there was a huge crowd - thousands of them. The unions made a call and peo-
10 ple just took off work. There were banners saying things like 'APARTHEID KILLS - KILL APARTHEID'. One group had banners with dozens and dozens of names - all of people killed by the police. But people weren't crying. They were angry, shouting
15 and singing. Some were even making the freedom shout, '**Amandla**', right in front of the tanks.

You should have seen how many policemen there were. They tried to say it was only for the family. But people just kept coming. However, we think the police
20 had orders not to shoot because there were so many TV cameras from overseas and reporters asking us questions.

Our lawyer is now pressing for an *inquiry*. I believe that those who beat me up are the same criminals who
25 shot my father.

We now live back in Soweto with my father's broth-er. Perhaps the police are going to make problems for us, but in the meantime Mma has got back her old job in Bara Hospital.
30 She sends you warmest greetings.

---

inquiry [ɪnˈkwaɪərɪ], here, the act of discovering and examining all the facts about something, especially a crime or an accident

There are big troubles in the schools here. Many students have been boycotting school for months and haven't taken their exams. In some schools armed soldiers are on patrol, even in the classrooms.

By the way, I've heard people mention the name of the friend you had here in Soweto. If it's the same person she is still locked up. They've got hundreds of us inside. Someone called prison the 'College of Politics', so now we talk here about going to 'University'!

Like my father always said, freedom lies at the end of a long road, and it's going to be a long struggle. Keep strong, Sis. I know you will.

Amandla!

Taolo

Naledi's heart burned. There were new links in the chain, binding her to people right here in this lonely place as well as to Taolo, to her imprisoned friend Grace and to so many others.

Each day the chain was growing longer and stronger. She was not alone. They were not alone. She had heard Rra Dikobe talk of 'the struggle' - and of sharing it. At first they had only been words to her. Now they were real.

She must show the picture and read Taolo's letter to others. Let them also feel the strength of the chain. Even Nono. There were still voices coming from outside Mma Tshadi's hut. Letter and picture in hand, Naledi hurried towards the gathering.

QUESTIONS

Chapter 1

1. Why was the man painting numbers on all the doors?
2. What did the villagers do when they heard about the move?
3. Why did they want to see Chief Sekete?

Chapter 2

1. Why did not Naledi go with the others?
2. Why did Naledi's mother work in the city away from her family?
3. What did her friend Grace write to her about?

Chapter 3

1. What did Naledi's grandmother do when she heard the news?
2. Why was not the white woman surprised?
3. What promise did she give to Nono?
4. What was the news about Boomdal?
5. Why was Mma Tshadi angry with Chief Sekete?

Chapter 4

1. What was the government's plan for people who speak Tswana?
2. What would happen to the others?
3. Why had the government told Saul Dikobe not to attend meetings?
4. What would the villagers' new houses be like?
5. What arrangements had been made for Chief Sekete and why?
6. Why will it be difficult for Naledi and Poleng to continue to be friends?

Chapter 5

1. How was Taolo Dikobe different from the other pupils?
2. Describe the headmaster's treatment of Taolo.
3. Explain why Taolo wanted to be with his father, even though he missed his friends in Soweto.
4. What does Taolo suggest they should do?

Chapter 6

1. What warning does the headmaster give the pupils?
2. What will happen to Mr Gwala?
3. What had happened to others living in Potchefstroom?
4. What does Mr Molaba do when he finds them discussing politics in the yard?

Chapter 7

1. How was Naledi punished by the headmaster?
2. How did he punish Taolo?
3. What threat did he make to Naledi?
4. What plan begins to form in Naledi's mind?

Chapter 8

1. What did the other children think about Naledi's beating?
2. Why did Chief Sekete leave the village in such a hurry?
3. What did Mma Tshadi ask Naledi to do?

Chapter 9

1. Why did Naledi go to see Mma Dikoba?
2. Describe Tiro's feelings when Naledi told him about the beating.

Chapter 10

1. What had happened to the chief's house?
2. Why did the police come to the village and what orders did they give?

Chapter 11

1. How did Nono defend Naledi against the policeman?
2. Why had the police taken David away?
3. Why was not Taolo also taken by the police?

Chapter 12

1. Why did the older students at school want to organise a prayer meeting?
2. How did the priest help them?
3. How did they succeed in getting the headmaster out of the way?
4. Explain how they elected five students to represent them.

Chapter 13

1. What plans did the 5 representatives make?

2. How did Naledi feel about getting involved?
3. Why was she not sure it was a good idea to let younger children take part?

Chapter 14

1. What news did Mma Dikobe have of her husband and son?
2. Explain the change of attitude towards Mma Dikobe.

Chapter 15

1. Describe the beginning of the march.
2. Explain what the police did.

Chapter 16

1. How did Mma Dikobe help Tiro?

Chapter 17

1. Why did the authorities close the school?
2. Why did not Naledi go into hiding?

Chapter 18

1. Why did Naledi go to the hospital?
2. What news did Mma Dikobe give her?

Chapter 19

1. What happened to their water?
2. What orders did the police give to Saul Dikobe?
3. What had happened to Taolo while he was in prison and what are his feelings now?
4. Explain Mma Tshadi's plan.
5. What had happened to David Sadire?

Chapter 20

1. When did the villagers realize that their situation was very serious?
2. What did the official say about their pension?

Chapter 21

1. Why did the Anti-Removal Committee come to the village?
2. What information makes it clear that Rra Thopi was spying for the government?
3. How had Nono's husband served his country and was he rewarded for that service?
4. Why were the children dependent on their grandmother's pension?

Chapter 22

1. Explain about the transport the B.Y.A. had organised.
2. What will the authorities do to break up the villagers' agreement?

Chapter 23

1. What did the villagers see on returning to the village?
2. Explain what happened at the magistrate's office.
3. How does Mma Dikobe give them hope?

Chapter 24

1. Explain the purpose of the letter to the minister.

Chapter 25

1. Why was there no water in the tap?
2. What happened to Taolo when they returned to the village?

Chapter 26

1. What arrangements were made to bring water to the village?
2. Why did Rra Thopi leave the meeting?
3. Describe what happened when the police came.

Chapter 27

1. Explain how Naledi felt about the situation.
2. How do the police take over?

Chapter 28

1. Which is the first house the bulldozer destroys?
2. Why hasn't the owner come out?
3. Who have come to buy the cattle?
4. How does Naledi feel when their house is destroyed along with the gardens of other houses?

Chapter 29

1. Describe the camp.
2. How does the villagers' story get into the paper?
3. Describe the local schools.
4. How does Naledi read the stories in the paper?

Chapter 30

1. How does Chief Sekete express his feelings?
2. Which new election is supported by Mma Tshadi?
3. Who is the letter to Naledi from and why is it so important?